"All Right. Out with It."

"I've seen th   mes
not to know
some sort of   w
what it is!"

"Well," said Lucy, "it's not a plan exactly, more like a passing thought, something which occurred to me as you went on and on about our local bad boy. . . ."

"Which is?" Margo prodded.

"He'd be ideal."

"For what?" Margo asked.

"A teacher." Lucy nodded. "You know, sort of a starter kit in the art of romance?" Impetuously, she raced on with the explanation before she could lose her nerve. "Think of it. He's got lots of experience, no emotional attachments, and you said yourself he must be very good at what he does. He'd be perfect!"

LAURIEN BLAIR

writes, "I am having a great time writing romances because they are one of the few places where you can construct a perfect world, and the ending is always happy. The other thing I hope readers will find in my books is a sense of fun. My characters are going to laugh a lot, love a lot and have a great time, for in the end, that's really what I think falling in love is all about."

Dear Reader:

SILHOUETTE DESIRE is an exciting new line of contemporary romances from Silhouette Books. During the past year, many Silhouette readers have written in telling us what other types of stories they'd like to read from Silhouette, and we've kept these comments and suggestions in mind in developing SILHOUETTE DESIRE.

DESIREs feature all of the elements you like to see in a romance, plus a more sensual, provocative story. So if you want to experience all the excitement, passion and joy of falling in love, then SILHOUETTE DESIRE is for you.

Karen Solem
Editor-in-Chief
Silhouette Books

LAURIEN BLAIR
Sweet Temptation

Silhouette Desire
Published by Silhouette Books New York
America's Publisher of Contemporary Romance

SILHOUETTE BOOKS, a Division of Simon & Schuster, Inc.
1230 Avenue of the Americas, New York, N.Y. 10020

Copyright © 1983 by Laurien Blair

Distributed by Pocket Books

ISBN: 0-671-49275-6

First Silhouette Books printing December, 1983

10 9 8 7 6 5 4 3 2 1

America's Publisher of Contemporary Romance

Printed in the U.S.A.

Sweet
Temptation

1

When the phone rang first thing Monday morning, Lucy Whitcomb was in no mood for small talk. She was hot, sweaty and tired; somewhere during the course of her just completed five-mile run, she had managed to misplace a sixty-pound dog. So far, it was not shaping up to be a good day.

Absently she plucked off the white terry-cloth sweatband that circled her head as she reached for the phone, her thoughts still centered on the missing animal, a black Standard poodle named Duncan, who was her constant companion. Where could he have gone? she wondered irritably, holding the receiver to her ear. He always made the morning run by her side, and he'd never wandered off before. To make matters worse, she'd been lost in thought, entranced by the bright beauty of Connecticut's autumn foliage, and had no idea at what point during the long run he'd decided to part company with her.

"Hello," she growled, her blue eyes straying to the large clock on the wall above the kitchen sink. Who the hell would have the nerve to be calling at seven-thirty in the morning anyway?

"Lucy Whitcomb?" the disembodied voice demanded, sounding none too pleased itself.

"Yes, this is she." Lucy sighed, mentally resigning herself to what was to come. Callers who checked her identity before stating their purpose were invariably selling something. What was it to be this time—insulation, magazine subscriptions, vacuum cleaners? Sometimes it seemed as though every solicitor with a product to hawk and a finger to dial had her number.

"My name is Simon Farlow, and we seem to have a mutual acquaintance."

Interesting, thought Lucy. That was certainly a new approach. Then she realized that the silence on the line was lengthening. Frowning thoughtfully, she turned the name over in her mind. Was it supposed to mean something to her? Lordy, he couldn't be her mother's best friend's nephew from Des Moines, could he? She'd been adamant on that point, no more blind dates! But then, when had her mother ever taken her wishes into consideration? No, Lucy remembered suddenly, his name had been Albert . . . Albert something . . .

"Miss Whitcomb, are you there?"

"Of course," Lucy snapped, chewing her lower lip in frustration. If only she didn't have such a terrible memory for names. Why didn't he just say what he wanted and get it over with?

Then he did, and it was the last thing she expected. "Well, I suggest that you hang up the phone and get over here—preferably as soon as possible. Thanks to you, Tess is going absolutely out of her mind with desire, and I don't relish the thought of listening to her lovesick moans any longer than I have to. I assume you've never tried to placate a bitch in heat, but believe me, it's no picnic."

Good God! Lucy blanched. Was this an obscene phone call? Now that she thought about it, she could hear the sound of heavy breathing going on in the background. But wasn't he supposed to be breathing into the phone? she wondered abstractedly. And who in the world was Tess? Just my luck, Lucy thought wryly. My first obscene phone call, and I don't even understand it!

Then reason reasserted itself, and she took the offensive. "Now you listen here, buddy—"

"Simon," the voice corrected decisively.

"Whoever," Lucy snapped, not about to give an inch. "What do you want?"

For a moment there was only silence on the line, as if the unknown caller was mentally counting to ten before he spoke. When he did, his voice was edged in steel. "What I want is for you to stop arguing," he said as though it were the most reasonable request in the world. "I live on Weed Street, it's just around the corner. How long will it take you to get here?"

"The rest of your life and then some," Lucy retorted, quite unable to believe that she was still caught up in this inane conversation. The man had to be crazy, which didn't say much for her mental faculties considering that she was still on the line talking to him. Hadn't she read somewhere that a whistle blown loudly into the receiver tended to discourage this sort of person from calling again?

Determinedly she strode across the small kitchen, stretching the telephone cord to its utmost. Cupping the receiver between her shoulder and her ear, she pulled open the junk drawer beside the refrigerator and rummaged through its assortment of odds and ends, looking for a noisemaker. To her disgust, the only thing she found that even came close was Duncan's silent dog whistle, whose tone was too high pitched for human ears and, judging by the poodle's lack of response the few times she had tried to use it, perhaps for his as well.

"Do you mean to say you're not going to do anything?" the voice demanded, and Lucy could well imagine the acrobatics he pictured her performing.

"Certainly not," she declared indignantly.

"Then you leave me no choice but to call the pound. I refuse to have my life disrupted this way!"

"The pound?" Lucy echoed faintly as realization began to dawn. "Do you mean the dog pound?"

"Is there another?" the voice shot back sarcastically.

"I suppose not," Lucy murmured, her interest in the conversation perking up considerably now that it was finally beginning to make some sense. "Does that mean you've found Duncan?"

"Are there any other dogs running around loose wearing tags with your name and number on them?" Simon Farlow asked drily.

"No," Lucy admitted slowly, pleased that he couldn't see the embarrassed flush that had begun to creep up over her cheeks. What an imagination! Thank God she hadn't blown a whistle in his ear.

"Then why else would you suppose that I'm calling at this ungodly hour of the morning?"

"Believe me," said Lucy, with a sudden, self-mocking grin, "you wouldn't want to know."

She took down directions to his house and two minutes later was behind the wheel of her bright red BMW 2002. Never a slow driver at the best of times, Lucy burnt rubber as she screeched out of the driveway, then made two right-hand turns, running both stop signs in the process but making it to Weed Street in record time. It wasn't until she had located Simon Farlow's address and found herself confronted by a soaring wood

12

and glass contemporary house on a large wooded lot that she spared the slightest thought for her appearance, and by then it was too late.

Impatiently she reached up to run her fingers through the tousled auburn curls framing her face, realizing with dismay how she must look. Her hair was limp and tangled after the long run and, having jumped straight out of bed and into her running clothes—a floppy, gray sweatshirt and a matching pair of old gray sweatpants— she was still this side of a much needed shower. On top of that, her face was damp with sweat and still flushed from the exertion. At least her eyes were bright and clear, thought Lucy, grasping unabashedly at straws. With their distinctive blue green color and abundant fringe of thick, dark lashes, they had always been her best feature. Today, they would simply have to stand on their own.

She parked her car at the top of the driveway and slipped out from behind the wheel, clutching suddenly at the oversized cotton pants as they chose that moment to remain behind, sliding quite far down her hips before she managed to get a firm grip on the waistband and hike them back up. Her slender body was almost lost beneath the voluminous folds of extra material. When she ran, the sweatsuit caught in the wind and billowed about her freely, giving her the appearance, as she jogged along the quiet back roads, of a low-flying Goodyear blimp.

There had been a time not so long ago, however, when she had needed all the extra room afforded by the large clothes, and then some. Fifteen months ago, just before her twenty-fifth birthday, she had tipped the scales at one hundred and seventy-five pounds. Lucy remembered the weigh-in well, for it had been a momentous occasion, and one that had prompted her to reevaluate her entire life. Even from her earliest childhood she had been overweight, having waged a continual, and losing, battle against food all her life. By the time she reached her adult height of five foot four, at the age of eighteen, she weighed one hundred and fifty pounds. Her father called her pleasantly plump. Her mother said she was solidly packed. But deep down inside, Lucy knew the real truth—she was just plain fat.

After a lifetime of playing the part of the jolly fat girl, she had found herself slipping automatically into the same role through four long years of college. Despite her best efforts, dormitory food had added substantially to her bulk, and by the time Lucy graduated, it had been months since she had dared to set foot on a scale. She'd tried and rejected one diet after another—the Scarsdale, the Stillman, the Beverly Hills. No fad was allowed to pass unnoticed, no miracle cure left unexplored. With slavish devotion, she drank water, ate grapefruit, spurned carbohydrates—only to see the small inroads she'd made disappear all too quickly in a flurry of compensatory eating, until she despaired of ever being thin and curled up in front of the TV to drown her sorrows in a tin of chocolate fudge brownies.

Her social life had suffered, of that there could be no doubt. Somehow it always seemed as though the men who were interested in her were the skinny, unattractive types, while the men whose eyes she would like to have caught basked in the adoration of petite, hopelessly slender Kewpie dolls. Not that Lucy was unduly worried. A true romantic at heart, she knew her knight in shining armor was out there somewhere. True love would strike, she was sure of it. It was only a matter of time.

In the meanwhile, she was left with more time and energy to devote to her career, which was coming along quite nicely. Her first two years out of college were spent working her way up from saleswoman to buyer in a fashionable Manhattan department store, learning the ins and outs of retailing from the ground up. Then a small bequest from her grandmother, added to her carefully hoarded savings and fostered by a small business loan from the bank, made a long-held dream come true. At the age of twenty-four, Lucy became her own boss when she opened "Sweet Tooth," her very own candy store, in the quiet suburban town of New Canaan, Connecticut.

With that move, however, what little self-control she'd formerly possessed seemed to evaporate. How could she possibly buy stock without sampling the candy first? she had asked herself, filled with self-righteous justification. And, more important, how could she expect her customers to indulge if she herself were abstentious?

Lucy knew she was in trouble when she outgrew her blue jeans for the third time in as many months. Already, all her skirts were wraparounds, her dresses flowing multihued caftans. Realistically she began to wonder, just how much further could she go? It was with dread foreboding that she went out and purchased a scale, only to discover when she tried to weigh herself that she was unable to see the dial around the bulk of her own body. That was the last straw.

The next day she had bought her first sweatsuit, and what started out as a brisk daily walk around the block had taken six months to evolve into her current five-mile run. A visit to a sympathetic doctor had armed her with a sensible diet plan and a system for counting calories she adhered to religiously, reveling in a diet that didn't demand she banish sweets from her life. As long as she remembered that a brownie used up two hundred calories from her daily allotment, or a Twinkie one hundred and fifty, she found it was still possible to indulge her cravings if she worked around them accordingly.

Little by little the pounds had melted away as Lucy marshaled willpower she'd never known she had.

Through good days and bad, through week-long pla-
teaus and irrational late-night binges, she persevered.
After six months, the first sweatsuit had been replaced by
another in a smaller size, then after that, another still, as
her body continued to shrink. Now, one year and three
months later, she was finally down to fighting weight and
had been for over a month. She was literally a mere
shadow of her former self—and life had never felt so
good.

With boundless enthusiasm, Lucy discovered long-
denied delights—shopping for lacy lingerie, buying a
bathing suit that actually fit, wearing clothes that suited
the way she felt about herself and not the matronly image
the garment industry had imposed upon her for so long.
The beginnings of a whole new wardrobe were already
hanging in her closet, and Lucy felt no shame at all over
her spree. Pampering herself with something other than
food was a new luxury to be savored and indulged to the
fullest.

With that thought in mind, she had spent an entire day
in a posh New York salon, emerging at dusk just in time to
catch the commuter train home, her russet hair newly
styled, her face shadowed and sculpted with cosmetics.
With childlike hope and wonder, she had put herself in
the hands of the experts; and even to her critical eye,
they had done an incredible job. Hair that had hung
limply halfway down her back now curled around her
head in riotous profusion. Bones that had been hidden
for so long now stood out clearly on the softly shaded
planes of her face. Finally, at the age of twenty-six, Lucy
knew she had come into her own.

So of course I *would* choose today of all days to go
jogging in my oldest clothes, she thought, her expression
halfway between a sigh and a scowl as she shaded her
eyes with her hand and looked up at the truly majestic
dwelling before her. Gray sweats and sneakers, just the

sort of attire one ought to wear when calling upon the lord of the manor.

Then, with a quick dismissive toss of her head, Lucy banished the thought. Squaring her shoulders determinedly, she marched around the house to the front door. What was she so worried about? After all, it wasn't as though she'd been invited to tea. The man didn't have to like her. All he had to do was to return her dog. So what did it matter what she looked like?

Which only went to prove, she thought a moment later, how wrong a person can be. Because when the door swung open and she was confronted by a man she could only assume to be Simon Farlow, her first impulse was to wish that she looked like anything other than what she did.

He was taller than she by at least six inches, a difference that her flat-soled sneakers only served to accentuate, and Lucy found herself gazing upward at a face that owed more of its charm to sheer rugged masculinity than to the vapid, boyish good looks so often termed handsome. The thatch of wheat blond hair hanging down over his ears had a casually mussed appearance, as though he had combed through the locks with his fingers, then never given them another thought. Dark, fathomless tawny brown eyes watched her curiously as she mentally catalogued the jutting planes of his high cheekbones, the strong slope of his jaw, the last vestiges of a lingering summer tan that gave his skin color and warmth.

A red plaid flannel shirt fit snugly across his broad shoulders, and the top two buttons were undone, revealing, Lucy noted thankfully, no gold chains, only more blond tendrils curling out through the opening. His faded jeans hugged a pair of hips and thighs that Lucy wouldn't have minded getting her hands on herself—slim, yet well rounded with the taut definition of well-toned muscles.

17

Idly she noted that his feet were encased in a pair of well-worn boots, and for some reason she knew, just by looking at him, that this was one man who had only himself to please.

Not bad, Lucy thought to herself, smiling with a connoisseur's appreciation for a fine physique. Not bad at all.

Women's lib notwithstanding, she had always been able to see why men were taken with a well-developed body, for she shared their enthusiasm; especially now, when exercise had become such a vital part of her own regime. Never again would she take such physical beauty for granted, thinking that it was something magically bestowed on a lucky few. No, there was nothing magical about it, she'd learned that. It was all a matter of dedication, determination and hard work. He may have started out with a few natural advantages, Lucy mused, but it was clear this was one man who made the most of what he had to work with. . . .

Abruptly her attention was brought back to the problem at hand by the appearance of her dog, who careened around Simon's legs and bolted out the front door between them to gambol crazily around the manicured front lawn. Watching him, Lucy realized that between her Bozo-the-clown attire and the antics of her poodle, they had probably given Simon Farlow a morning he wouldn't forget for a long time. Quickly she stifled an unseemly desire to laugh out loud. It was probably good for him, she decided smugly. Anyone who looked that self-assured deserved to have his life shaken up every now and again.

Hearing the sound of a throat being cleared softly behind her, Lucy swung her attention back to the man in the doorway, only to discover that his eyes were roaming over her with a desultory, almost derisive negligence.

18

Instinctively she knew that she had been weighed and found wanting, and the first words out of his mouth did nothing to dispel that impression.

"You look," he said by way of a greeting, "like the 'before' woman in an ad for an exercise gym."

Abruptly Lucy felt all her old insecurities begin to slip back into place, their oppressive weight settling over her like a shroud. Then, with a stubborn, outward thrust of her chin, she banished them just as quickly as they had come. She could hold her own with any man, including this one. What sort of thing was that to say to a total stranger anyway? Hadn't his mother taught him any manners?

"Thank you very much," she replied tartly, glowering up at him. "If you think this is bad, you should see me on an off day."

"Worse than that?" Simon Farlow shook his head sympathetically, although Lucy was sure she could detect just the faintest gleam of laughter in his eyes.

"Much worse," she confirmed, with a reckless grin, declining to elaborate. Let him use his imagination!

"Thank God for small favors," Simon muttered, his gaze sweeping over her from head to toe once more as he frowned in disbelief. "Are you sure there's really only one of you in there?"

"Quite." Lucy was taken by surprise as he reached out to grasp the soft cotton top between thumb and forefinger and pulled it away from her body, watching as it continued to stretch for a good foot and a half. "Hey!" she cried, outraged. "What do you think you're doing?"

The act of jumping back was purely reflex. Immediately Simon released his hold, and the sweatshirt redraped itself in soft folds around her torso as a cheery grin creased his face. "That's the damnedest thing I've ever seen. Who designs your clothes, Omar the Tentmaker?"

"Who designs yours," Lucy snapped in quick retaliation, her eyes darting from the boots to the jeans to the braided leather belt that circled his waist, "the Marlboro man?"

"Touché, Miss Whitcomb," Simon said, inclining his head graciously, the corners of his eyes crinkling in amusement.

"Lucy," she corrected automatically, the other form of address having always made her feel like a spinster schoolteacher or somebody's maiden aunt.

Idly she noticed that the smile had transformed his face, warming his features in a way that made him look much more approachable—and very, very interesting. Just my luck, she thought with a small, silent sigh. The most exciting man I've seen in months and I have to show up on his front doorstep dressed like a clown. Even worse, he has the nerve to call me on it. Lucy girl, who are you trying to kid?

"Simon Farlow," he announced, holding out his hand.

"So I'd guessed," Lucy said, pursing her lips in a rueful smile as the humor of the situation got the better of her. She extended her hand as well and found her fingers engulfed in a warm, strong clasp.

"I hope Duncan didn't cause you too much trouble," she said, withdrawing her hand reluctantly and turning around to check on her dog's whereabouts. "He left while we were out jogging, and it wasn't until I got home that I noticed that he was missing." She looked disparagingly at the poodle, who was posing and preening in the front yard. "As you can see, he has quite a high opinion of himself. I'm sure he thought you'd be quite thrilled to have him as a visitor. It hasn't yet dawned on him that not everyone finds him as irresistible as he finds himself."

At that, Simon chuckled as he stepped out onto the porch and pulled the front door carefully shut behind him. "If that's the way he feels, I'm afraid this morning's visit will have done nothing to change his mind. Tess found him to be utterly fascinating."

Lucy had been halfway down the front steps on the way to retrieve her errant dog, but the mention of that name brought her up short. So much so, in fact, that Simon, who had been following right behind, was taken totally by surprise. His upraised knee caught her squarely in the seat of the pants and knocked her forward, sending her stumbling down the last two steps, mentally cursing her clumsiness as she fell.

In an instant, he had leapt down beside her, his arms shooting out to grasp her shoulders and save her from total ignominy. For an awful moment, Lucy imagined that her weight would send them both crashing to the ground anyway. Then she became aware that his long, lean fingers were encircling her upper arms easily, and remembered. Effortlessly, Simon supported her, steadying her on her feet until she stepped back out of his grasp, an embarrassed apology forming on her lips.

"Sorry about that. My fault entirely," Simon said quickly, beating her to it, and Lucy marveled at the way the simple words managed to dispel her feelings of awkwardness. If he wanted to take the blame, who was she to argue with him?

"If you say so," she agreed, smiling up at him easily, her cobalt eyes alight with rampant curiosity. "Tell me," she demanded, "who is Tess?"

"Champion Far Hill's Shining Hour," Simon informed her, with a trace of what Lucy could almost swear was paternal pride. "She's my dog, a golden retriever bitch who is, at the moment, very much in season. So you see, it wasn't willful disobedience on Duncan's part that brought him here, but rather the most basic of nature's instinctual responses."

"Oh," Lucy said, assimilating this information in light of their earlier conversation over the phone.

"Not that I think that excuses the fact that your poodle was out running loose," Simon continued, frowning. "Have you no sense of responsibility at all? Don't you realize that dogs who are allowed to run free are fair game for dognappers, not to mention a potential traffic hazard and a nuisance for your neighbors? If I were you," he said sternly as though delivering a lecture to a recalcitrant child, "I would invest in a leash and make use of it."

"How dare you?" Lucy's immediate protest was vehement and automatic. "Who gave you the right to decide whether or not my dog is well treated?"

"You did," Simon maintained, unperturbed, "when you allowed him to find his way into my yard. Use whatever means you wish to control your dog, but see that you do it. In the future, I would not like to find him hanging around here again."

"Believe me, you won't," Lucy sputtered angrily, amazed at how quickly the mood of easy affability had managed to dissolve. Blue eyes shooting fire, she marched over to where Duncan stood and grasped him firmly by the collar.

"Good." Simon nodded to himself, the matter obviously having been settled to his satisfaction. "You asked me a question, now it's my turn to ask you one. Is there any particular reason why you're dressed like a mummy?"

For a moment the rapid change of subject left Lucy quite speechless. Then, in a rush of anger at him, at herself, and most of all at the ludicrous situation in which she found herself, her voice returned. "You, Mr. Simon Farlow, have been nothing but rude since I arrived," she cried, turning upon him to vent the full range of her ire.

"So I'll answer your question in the same spirit in which it was asked—it's none of your damned business!"

With that, she strode over and jerked open the front door to the BMW and whistled Duncan inside. Climbing in beside him, she slammed the door with a satisfyingly loud thud, then roared off down the driveway without so much as a backward glance.

2

Quite predictably Lucy was late for work, and all the hurrying in the world didn't seem to make the slightest bit of difference. Once home, she hustled Duncan safely inside, then dashed for the bathroom and a hot shower, pulling off her sweatshirt as she ran, and leaving a trail of discarded clothing in her wake. The quick shower was followed by an even quicker change of clothing as Lucy pulled open the closet door and put on the first thing that came to hand, a gray wool tweed skirt and matching vest, with a white ruffled blouse underneath. When she jabbed a fingernail through her last pair of stockings, she tossed aside the pumps she'd been planning to wear and zipped on a pair of knee-high black leather boots instead.

In the kitchen she quickly mixed Duncan's food, watching with satisfaction and not a small amount of envy as he wolfed the bowlful down, then set a pot of tea to brew for herself. While it heated, she applied her makeup and brushed her hair, then raced back to the kitchen to toss down a quick cup of tea, lemon no sugar, and decided to call it breakfast.

Nevertheless it was still well past nine o'clock by the time she eased the BMW into the small parking space behind the store. "It's a good thing I'm the boss," she muttered aloud to no one in particular, and Duncan obligingly cocked an ear to listen. Holding him by a firm grip on the collar, she tried the back door and found it unlocked, indicating that her assistant, Margo Leeds, had already arrived.

"Is that you, Luce?" came the high-pitched girlish voice from up front as Lucy let herself in, and the small bells above the door jangled noisily.

"Who were you expecting, the sweet-tooth fairy?" Lucy teased as she released Duncan's collar, and the poodle trotted in to lie down on the small bed she had fashioned for him in a corner of her office. Closing the door behind him, she walked down the hall to join Margo in the shop. "Sorry I'm late. It's just been one of those mornings."

"I'll let you get away with it this time," said Margo, planting her hands on her hips and frowning with mock severity, "but see that you don't make a habit of it."

"Yes, ma'am," Lucy replied meekly, tossing her friend a snappy salute, then lowering her hand to stifle an unexpected yawn.

Whereas Lucy was small and fair, Margo was just the opposite, standing one inch under six feet, with olive-toned skin and long, glossy black hair. Slender almost to the point of being skinny, she was the only person Lucy knew who could eat everything in sight and never gain an ounce. If they hadn't been such good friends, Lucy could easily have hated her.

"Late night last night?" said Margo, raising one eyebrow inquiringly before turning back to the tins of butter mints she was stacking on a shelf.

"Hardly." Lucy shook her head. "Early morning."

"That running of yours gets you up early every morning." Margo groaned. "I don't see how you do it. All I can say is you've got more willpower than I do." Turning, she glowered at her boss, who was eying the large display case of Godiva chocolates in the rear of the store longingly. Having been Lucy's friend and co-worker for over a year, she was well aware of the battle of the bulge that had been waged and won. "And speaking of willpower, don't you dare!"

"I'm just looking." Lucy sniffed. "Besides, I didn't have time to eat any breakfast."

"Breakfast," Margo informed her succinctly, "consists of such things as cereal and eggs, and perhaps in the case of a dire emergency, jelly doughnuts, but never, let me repeat *never*, Godiva chocolates." Grinning, she rolled her eyes heavenward as if seeking divine guidance. "How you can even *look* at those things at this hour of the morning is beyond me."

"Bite your tongue!" Lucy cried, outraged. "Considering your profession, that's a horrible attitude to have. Didn't anyone ever tell you there's no such thing as a wrong time for chocolate? Breakfast, lunch, dinner—"

"Coffee break, midnight snack, four a.m. . . . ." Margo supplied helpfully.

"Now you're getting the idea." Lucy nodded approvingly, refusing to rise to the bait.

Walking over to the gleaming glass counter near the door, she flicked away an imaginary piece of dust, then turned to survey the rest of the store with a loving eye, checking automatically to make sure everything was in perfect order. Thinking back, she remembered the first time she had seen the small shop, then the drab, dreary office of a none-too-successful accountant. A good cleaning and a fresh coat of ivory paint had worked wonders, and that was only the beginning.

Now, bright mirror-covered walls provided the perfect backdrop for the rows of shelves displaying her wares. Large, clear crystal jars were filled to the brim with a mouth-watering selection of colorful candies—everything from spearmint leaves to jelly beans to lollipops. Beneath the shelves stood two glass display cases where the chocolates were arrayed in solitary splendor, and beside them the newest addition, a freezer filled with Italian ices in exotic flavors.

On hot summer days Lucy left the door propped open invitingly, and the bright, cheery store had become a gathering place for shopping matrons and their children as well. Her initial bank loan well under control, she was now thinking in terms of expansion, her sights set on having an ice cream and soda parlor under the "Sweet Tooth" banner as well.

"Where's Duncan?" Margo asked suddenly, realizing that the poodle hadn't followed his mistress into the shop. "Didn't you bring him in with you?"

"Of course, he's here," said Lucy. "You know this place is his second home as well as mine. He'd sulk for days if I ever left him behind. At the moment, however, he's in the doghouse, so to speak. I've locked him in my office to give him a chance to think over his sins."

Casually she inched her way along the counter, sliding stealthily closer and closer to the Godivas.

"Do you mean wonder dog actually did something wrong?" Margo said, pretending to be horrified since she knew the high regard in which Lucy normally held her pet.

"Not wrong exactly, just inconvenient," Lucy explained, gaining another foot and a half. "It seems there's a bitch in season in the neighborhood, and Duncan was the first to discover her."

"A fact with which her owner wasn't too pleased?" Margo guessed, fully aware of Lucy's furtive movements, but choosing for the moment to ignore them.

"That's putting it mildly. The way Simon Farlow lit into me when I went to pick Duncan up, you'd think the guillotine was too mild a punishment!"

"Simon Farlow?" Margo echoed, her voice squeaky with surprise. "*The* Simon Farlow?"

"I suppose so," said Lucy with studied indifference. "Unless you know of more than one?"

"Not likely!"

"Thank God," Lucy replied fervently as she slipped the long, slender fingers of one hand into the back of the display case. "One man like that is more than enough."

"I take it you weren't wildly impressed?" Margo arched one full eyebrow delicately upward.

"Should I have been?"

"Well," Margo said slowly, considering her answer. "Let's just say there are any number of women in New Cannan who wouldn't mind having a run-in with the great man himself." Out of the corner of one eye, she watched as Lucy succeeded in snaring a large, chocolate-covered praline.

"Great man?" Lucy echoed curiously, forgetting her candy for the moment as she straightened and stared at her friend. "What are you talking about?"

"Well, maybe not great exactly," Margo allowed, "but certainly famous. And by the way," she added, nodding significantly at Lucy's cupped hand, "I saw that."

"Slave driver," Lucy muttered under her breath, ignoring her assistant's frown and popping the confection in her mouth. "Did anyone ever tell you you're no fun?"

"Never," Margo declared airily.

"Good," said Lucy, speaking with her mouth full as she savored the morsel to the fullest. "Then don't start now." She swallowed dramatically, then continued with the conversation. "So tell me, aside from his obvious physical attributes, which are, I will admit, the stuff of which greatness is made, what is Simon Farlow famous for?"

"He's an architect," Margo explained, looking pointedly at her friend's hips as though waiting for a lump the size of the praline to appear. "You know, world renowned and all that."

"Really?" Lucy said thoughtfully. "I've never heard of him."

Margo's dark eyes twinkled mischievously. "I'm not sure that's entirely relevant. How many architects *have* you heard of?"

"Plenty," Lucy shot back, then immediately wished she hadn't.

"Go on," Margo challenged, folding her arms over her chest. "I'm waiting."

Quickly Lucy searched her memory. "Frank Lloyd Wright?"

"That's one," Margo allowed, raising one finger and wiggling it back and forth for encouragement.

"Le Corbusier?" Lucy offered hopefully.

"Two." Margo held aloft a second digit. "Now try for someone a little more modern."

"I. M. Pei?"

"Will wonders never cease?" Margo mused aloud, looking at her boss in pleased surprise as she held up a third finger. "You're getting warmer. Keep going."

"I can't," Lucy said with a quick, perplexed shrug. "That's it. We've exhausted my knowledge of the subject."

"And to think you call yourself a college graduate," Margo teased, shaking her head.

"In business, not liberal arts," Lucy bantered back, her

cobalt eyes taking on a wicked gleam. "Lord knows we can't all be debutantes—you know, budding young society matrons with nothing to do but study art and philosophy?"

"That's a cheap shot!" cried Margo, pretending to take offense although she knew Lucy meant no harm. "I may have been a debutante when I was eighteen, but now I work just as hard as anybody else."

"Really?" Lucy teased, getting some of her own back. "I haven't seen any evidence of that this morning."

"Who was the one who was late?" Margo demanded, her eyes round with innocence.

"I told you, that wasn't my fault."

"Tell it to the marines," Margo retorted, grinning broadly. "All I know is that sometime between last night and this morning you managed to meet Simon Farlow, New Canaan's own Casanova, and then you show up for work not only late, but yawning as well. Just think what kind of juicy tales I could weave out of that!"

"Okay, okay." Lucy laughed, holding up her hands, palms out, in a gesture of surrender. "I know when I'm beaten. Don't you dare go pairing me off with that man!"

"Tut, tut." Margo shook her head. "Don't be so hasty, my dear. You could do worse, you know."

"Not necessarily," Lucy retorted. "No wonder he's still single. If that man's as rude to everyone else as he was to me this morning, I can see why no woman would want him."

"Oh, they want him all right," Margo declared. "From what I hear, he's scored quite a hit with the ladies in town."

"Is that so?" said Lucy, leaning forward to listen as curiosity got the better of her. "Do tell."

Margo sighed dramatically. "For a smart, savvy woman, Lucy, you are dreadfully uninformed. Don't you know that in small towns, everyone is supposed to know everyone else's business? What's the matter with you, have you spent your whole life with your head in the sand?"

"No," Lucy quipped, "in the refrigerator. Now go on. Don't keep me in suspense. I want to know everything."

"I don't know *everything*," Margo protested halfheartedly, but she set aside the tins she had been shelving and hoisted herself up into a comfortable position atop the display case, settling in for a long chat. "Although the bits and pieces I do know are really quite something . . ."

As she spoke, Lucy relaxed back against the counter, propping her elbows on its top for support. Her features settled into a thoughtful frown as she listened in rapt fascination to the tales of Simon's exploits, picturing him in her mind's eye the way she had first seen him that morning—tall, broad-shouldered, compellingly confident and totally, utterly male. He might have his faults, she had certainly discovered that this morning, but there was no denying that he had a definite brand of appeal as well. Yes, thought Lucy, Simon Farlow was an enormously attractive man. In fact, if she were to be honest with herself, he was just the sort of man she wouldn't mind cutting her newfound teeth on. . . .

Subtly and quite without warning, an idea began to take shape in the back of her mind, an idea so outrageous that it was a moment or two before she gave it any credence at all. Then the very thought brought a deliciously wicked smile to her lips and she wondered whether or not she might be able to pull it off.

". . . and then, as I heard it, Simon slipped out the second-story window and climbed down the trellis, just as her husband was coming in the—" Abruptly Margo broke off her recital when she noticed the odd expression on her friend's face. "Lucy Whitcomb, are you listening to me? I'm not telling these stories for my benefit, you know. I don't believe you've heard a single word I've said!"

"Of course I have," Lucy said soothingly while she did her best to keep a straight face.

"All right, out with it," Margo demanded. "I've seen that gleam in your eye too many times not to know what it means. You're hatching up some sort of diabolical plan, and I want to know what it is!"

"Well," said Lucy, hedging, as she decided how much she wanted to reveal, "it's not a plan exactly, more like a passing thought, something that occurred to me as you went on and on about our local bad boy. . . ."

"Which is?" Margo prodded. It was like pulling teeth.

Lucy straightened and turned to face the counter behind her, neatening the already immaculate display. "He'd be perfect."

"For what?" Margo delicately arched one eyebrow upward.

Lucy mumbled something inaudible under her breath.

"What?" Margo said, leaning closer. "I didn't hear you."

At that, Lucy pivoted on her heel, thrusting her chin out stubbornly as if daring her friend to defy her. "A teacher."

"A teacher?" Margo echoed faintly, her expression one of bewilderment.

Lucy nodded. "You know, sort of a starter kit in the art of romance?" Impetuously she raced on with the explanation before she lost her nerve. "Think of it. He's got lots of experience, no emotional attachments, and you yourself said he must be very good at what he does. He'd be perfect!"

In spite of herself, Margo began to giggle at the absurdity of the idea. "You can't be serious!"

"Oh, but I am," said Lucy, becoming surer and surer

of herself by the moment as the idea took root and began to grow. "This isn't the nineteen fifties, you know. Men aren't the only ones doing the pursuing anymore." Defiantly, she planted her hands on her hips. "And you don't have to look so shocked either! Remember the sexual revolution?"

"Of course," Margo said warily, not at all sure she liked the direction the conversation was taking. "But that doesn't mean I was out there on the front lines!"

Lucy grinned. "Maybe not," she allowed, "but knowing you, I'll bet you were back in the ranks somewhere."

"I was, and that's where you should be as well. Back in the ranks, feeling your way slowly—not jumping in over your head on the first attempt!"

Lucy frowned impatiently. "You don't understand what it's like. I've been sitting on the sidelines for nearly all of my life. Well, that's over now, and it's my turn to howl. Besides," she insisted, "I'm going to approach the whole thing logically and rationally. I won't be getting in over my head at all because I'll know exactly what I'm doing every step of the way."

"Spoken like a true romantic," said Margo, teasingly. "I thought you were the one who was waiting for true love—you know, Mr. Right, the knight on the white charger who was going to sweep you off your feet?"

"I am," Lucy maintained, blithely ignoring the contradiction. "And when the time comes, I know just how it will be. Our eyes will meet across a crowded room, our hearts will beat as one. Like kindred souls who have found each other at last, we will know, right that very moment, that we were made for one another."

Then the dreamy, faraway look in her eyes faded. "But what has one thing got to do with the other?" she demanded. "I'm twenty-six years old, and I've been waiting for true love a long time. So he isn't Mr. Right. Who says I shouldn't get a little experience in the meantime? That way, when my knight does come along, I'll be ready.

"It's not enough just to recognize him for what he is," she pointed out. "In this day and age, I'll need to know what to do with him as well. That old saying 'the way to a man's heart is through his stomach' may have been true in our mothers' time, but not anymore. Now there's a more scenic route to take, and I'm just going to let Simon Farlow clue me in to a few of the landmarks, that's all."

"You're crazy," said Margo, shaking her head. "Fully and certifiably insane. This is the looniest idea I've ever heard. And aside from everything else, what makes you so sure that Simon will agree to take part?"

"Why wouldn't he?" Lucy said airily, with far more confidence than she felt. "From what you tell me, the man chases anything in a skirt. He's been using women all his life. Well now, for a change, the shoe will be on the other foot." With a wry, self-mocking frown, she looked down over her body. "Besides, I can't imagine he'll find the going too arduous."

Across the room, Margo was still shaking her head. Deliberately she hopped down from her perch, walked over and peered closely into Lucy's face. "Are you sure you're feeling all right?"

Taking the rhetorical question for what it was, Lucy declined to answer as, her thoughts far away, she mused aloud, "Of course there are a few small details that need working out. I'll have to make him forget he ever met Bozo the clown . . ."

Margo's eyes opened wide, but the startled response she was about to make was cut short when the sweet, tinkling sound of the small bells above the front door announced the arrival of their first customer of the day, effectively signaling an end to the conversation.

Lucy banished all thoughts of Simon Farlow from her mind and slipped back into her professional, businesslike persona. It was time to go to work. Intriguing as the man was, she would have to worry about him another time.

Leaving Margo out front to cope, Lucy went back down the hall to her office, intent on tackling the mounds of paperwork on her desk, which never seemed to go away no matter how diligently she applied herself to their disposal. As things turned out, between making out orders, doing the bills, unpacking deliveries and talking to visiting salesmen, she was kept so busy for the rest of the day that she didn't spare Simon another thought until six-thirty the following morning when it was time for her run.

His presence was brought to mind by the sudden realization that if Duncan was to jog with her, she would have to come up with a leash of some sort, for he certainly couldn't be trusted to maintain his position by her side unaided. Swearing under her breath at the inconsideration of neighbors whose bitches came into season and disrupted her carefully ordered life, Lucy launched a fifteen-minute search, finally managing to scare up an old leather lead she found twined around a doorknob in the garage.

"Sorry about this," she said to the dog while she snapped one end onto his collar and looped the other around her wrist. Duncan looked at her balefully through large, sad eyes. "I'm afraid you just can't fight Mother Nature."

Then they were out the door and down the driveway, shuffling through the crisp, ankle-deep leaves she had yet to rake up, as they made their way to the road and settled into a steady, even pace. Drawing a deep breath, Lucy laughed aloud in pure enjoyment, delighting in the solid, responsive action of her well-toned muscles and the invigorating touch of the cold, early-morning air on her cheeks and throat. There was something about running that always made her feel uniquely alive, as though she were filled with limitless energy. Petty, everyday worries slipped away like the breeze that surrounded her. When she ran, she was invincible!

This was the time of the day Lucy liked the best, when the whole world seemed to be hers alone as it came awake around her. Her eyes wide with wonder, she took in the constantly changing kaleidoscope of colors of the autumn leaves, a sight she had seen many times before, but one that never failed to delight her with its timeless beauty. From palest yellow to deep, rich red and all the colors of the spectrum in between, the trees had donned their fall finery in a final bid for glory before surrendering to the cold, stark winter that followed.

This was a time that was all Lucy's own—to think, to plan, to dream. In the past, she had conceived some of her best ideas while out running. Today, however, with unnerving predictability, her thoughts centered themselves firmly on the man of the hour, Mr. Simon Farlow. She hadn't been kidding when she'd told Margo there were still some minor details to be worked out, Lucy thought wryly. It was one thing to decide that you were going to be the local Lothario's latest lady, quite another to pull it off. If only she hadn't put her foot in it so badly yesterday! First showing up on his doorstep looking like something the cat dragged in, and then yelling at the man like a shrew. Not that it hadn't been mostly his own fault anyway. Talk about nerve!

Then again, Lucy decided, there wasn't any reason why she couldn't be big about the whole thing and assume most of the blame. Perhaps that was the best way to go. She could call and apologize, maybe offer to buy him a drink and make amends? Nodding to herself, Lucy pictured the scene with satisfaction. This time she would be totally in control. There would be no wayward poodle, no oversized sweatsuit, no disheveled appearance to cause her any embarrassment. She would be witty and charming and utterly sophisticated. And Simon Farlow would never know what had hit him. It could work, she thought determinedly. She'd make it work!

This time, she arrived back home on schedule with poor Duncan still reluctantly in tow. There was time for a proper shower and breakfast as well, and she still managed to beat Margo to the shop by a full fifteen minutes. But for a day that had started out in a perfectly ordinary way, somehow by noon, it seemed to have lost all semblance of reality. First there was the phone call from a major supplier with the news that they had yet to receive an order she had sent six weeks ago. Did she wish to receive another shipment or not? Paling at the thought, for her supplies were already rather low and she had counted on that shipment being already on the way, Lucy snatched up a pad and pencil and hurried into the storeroom to do a quick inventory.

No sooner had she finished there, however, than a deliveryman managed to drop three cartons of the delicate ribbon candy she had ordered for the upcoming holiday season, turning the graceful loops into a mass of tiny shards and splinters. His muttered reassurance that the candy would taste the same no matter what it looked like did nothing to mollify her, and it was just about this time that Margo approached with the news that Duncan had slipped out the front door in the wake of an incoming customer.

"Blast, blast and double blast!" Lucy swore, kicking one of the battered cartons on the floor in disgust. Now she would have to go out and bring the poodle back, and there was little doubt in her mind where he would head. The call of the wild strikes, again, she thought irritably, frowning as she remembered Simon's adamant warning to keep her dog under control. One lapse was bad enough, but two less than a day apart? Lucy shuddered. He'd never forgive that. Didn't that dumb dog realize he was playing havoc with all her plans?

Stopping only long enough to snatch up her car keys from her desk, Lucy dashed out the back door of the shop. With any luck, she could overtake the poodle with the BMW, "cutting him off at the pass" before he had a chance to do any plaintive wailing outside of Tess's window.

Luck, however, wasn't with her, for she didn't spot Duncan at all during the speedy seven-minute drive. More than likely, his unerring nose had guided him across the overland route, through hedges and streams and neighbors' yards, for when the red BMW shot full speed ahead into Simon's driveway, Lucy immediately saw that the dog had beaten her there, somewhat dirty and a little bedraggled, but otherwise none the worse for wear.

She quickly hopped out of the car and started across the lawn after him, the fashionably high heels of her lizard pumps digging into the turf with every step she took. A furtive glance at the house out of the corner of her eye told her nothing of the owner's whereabouts. Maybe he wasn't even home, Lucy decided hopefully. Surely architects had offices or somewhere to go during the day, didn't they? In any case, he hadn't noticed them as yet. If only Duncan would come on the first call, things might still be all right. She could bundle him into the car, then coast back down the driveway like a thief in the night. Simon need never even know he'd had visitors.

"Duncan," she called softly, holding out her hand as if offering a treat, "come here, boy. Come on."

The response she got had nothing at all in common with the one she wanted. The poodle looked her straight in the eye, then planted his feet firmly where he stood and turned his muzzle upward into the wind to give a long, low howl—the mating call, canine style.

"Stop it! Cut that out!" cried Lucy, glaring at the dog in horror. To her immense relief, several moments passed and no answering yelp came from within. "Your lady love isn't home. Now get over here, you. Duncan, come!" Her best obedience-school tone had no effect whatsoever as Duncan, seemingly unperturbed by the lack of a response, simply repeated the performance, this time louder.

With an eloquence born of frustration, Lucy swore loudly and vehemently as a series of involuntary shivers racked her slender body. It was only then it occurred to her that, in her haste, she had left her coat behind in the shop. Her dress, a beautiful paisley silk in muted fall shades of burgundy, rust and taupe, was a triumph of fashion over function and offered scant protection against the chill, late September air.

"Duncan," she growled, her teeth gritted tightly together to keep them from chattering. "Get over here this instant!"

At that the poodle swung around, but Lucy's rising hopes were quickly dashed when he turned and trotted purposefully away in the other direction. With little choice but to follow, she did, while vague thoughts of a flying tackle ran through her mind. Rounding the back of the house, they found themselves on the edge of a large meadow, and Duncan put on a sudden burst of speed.

"No!" Lucy cried, exasperated almost to the point of tears. "Come back here!"

Perhaps it was the desperation in her voice that reached him, but this time Duncan did more than look her way, he turned and galloped toward her, as if at last the game was finally over. At the last moment, however, he dodged neatly to one side, avoiding her outstretched hand and dancing quite happily just out of reach. Lucy's forward lunge only sent him skittering several steps backward as he began a new sort of game, always careful to keep a safe distance between them.

"If I ever catch you, I'm going to make poodle stew," Lucy muttered under her breath while Duncan feinted first to the right and then to the left, enjoying her obvious frustration.

A long, low whistle coming from somewhere behind her back was the first thing that alerted Lucy to the fact that she and Duncan were no longer alone. Immediately, the poodle's ears pricked in response, his eyes drawn to a spot just behind her left shoulder, and with a sinking feeling somewhere in the region of her stomach, she knew what it was that he saw. So much for the best-laid plans, Lucy thought with a small sigh, knowing full well that all her ideas for a carefully orchestrated second meeting had just flown straight out the window. Damn, this wasn't how things were supposed to go at all!

Slowly, she pivoted where she stood, stalling for time and hoping against hope that she could think of a suitable rejoinder in the few seconds she had left. She wanted to say something terribly clever or, barring that, passably witty. Even snappy would have done in a pinch. In fact, she'd have settled for almost anything that would have drawn Simon's attention away from the fact that the dog he had warned her about yesterday was once more engaged in running about his yard. Unfortunately, nothing of that nature came to mind.

Instead, as she turned around, Lucy found herself struck quite speechless by the unexpected sight that greeted her. The reason for their discovery became immediately clear—the back wall of Simon Farlow's house was constructed entirely of glass! From where she stood, it seemed to sparkle with the brilliance of an enormous gem as the soft autumn sun slanted off the large panes. Slowly Lucy drew in her breath in a gasp of wonder. It was magnificent!

A long moment passed before she even remembered Simon's presence. Then she saw that he was standing in the middle of a wide wooden deck, which ran along the whole length of the house. Her eyes skimmed over him, noting that he was dressed much the same way he had been the day before, in jeans, boots and a washed-out, faded denim shirt. Then Lucy's active imagination took over, and she realized that, standing above her as he was, with the sun reflecting off the glass behind him, picking up the lights in his blond hair and illuminating the physical perfection of his body, he looked like some sort of primitive god. Apollo perhaps, Lucy thought fancifully, god of the sun.

"It has that effect on people sometimes," Simon said softly, watching her reaction. "I've lived here for five years, but sometimes, when I catch it in just the right light, it can still take my breath away."

"Glorious," Lucy breathed in awe, without stopping to examine whether she was referring to the house or its owner. "Positively glorious."

Then the spell surrounding them was broken when Duncan decided it was time to sound his mating call once more, and the sound of a plaintive, mournful howl filled the yard.

"Oh, for Pete's sake!" Lucy frowned, her face flushing a bright shade of crimson as she turned to confront the dog. "Cut out that racket, will you?"

Duncan cast her a baleful look and went on with his serenade.

"Shhh," crooned Simon, and immediately the howling stopped as the poodle wagged his tail happily, then galloped past Lucy and jumped onto the deck. Simon reached out a hand in greeting, and the dog sidled over, pressing himself against the man's thighs as though they were old friends.

"Sorry, old boy," Simon said, looking down at the poodle solemnly. "I'm afraid all your efforts are in vain today. Tess isn't here anymore. I shipped her off to Colorado to be bred."

"Colorado?" Lucy repeated incredulously as she glowered up at her traitorous dog. How was it that between the two of them, they'd managed to make her feel like the outsider? "Aren't there any male golden retrievers in Connecticut?"

"Of course," Simon said easily. "But the dog Tess has been sent to isn't just any golden retriever. Actually, he's the top Sporting Dog in the country."

"How nice for him," Lucy murmured, not having even the slightest idea what it was he was talking about. How had her dog and that man managed to become such good friends so quickly? Two against one, she thought irritably, and decided it was time to exert some control over the situation.

"Duncan, come!" she said firmly, slapping her thigh, an action that under normal circumstances would have brought the poodle scampering to her side. Much to her annoyance, however, Duncan made not the slightest move to comply, obviously preferring Simon's company to her own. Belatedly, and with no small amount of embarrassment, Lucy realized that if she wanted the poodle, she was going to have to climb up onto the deck and retrieve him.

"I take it Duncan isn't trained," Simon commented, watching the interplay with ill-concealed amusement.

"To do what?" Lucy asked irritably, switching her glare from the dog to the man without missing a beat.

"Anything," Simon said drily.

"Of course he's trained," Lucy said, defending her

animal. "It's just that sometimes he likes to assert his independence."

"Just like his owner, I suspect."

Lucy quickly bit back the retort that sprang to her lips, remembering just in time that she wanted to charm the man, not antagonize him. "You may be right," she purred, climbing the two steps to join them on the deck. Deliberately, she pursed her lips into what she hoped was a sultry-looking pout. "Once again, it seems I must apologize for my dog's behavior. I'd tell you it won't happen again, but I'm afraid I've already tried that once."

"Please," said Simon, responding with a warm, ever so engaging smile, "don't apologize. It isn't every day that I look up from my worktable to find a wood nymph cavorting about my back yard."

His deep brown eyes ran appreciatively over the soft curves of her figure, which were covered but hardly concealed by the clinging silk, and Lucy was shocked to realize that the power of his gaze touched her as surely as any caress. From the slender, shapely line of her calves to the slight flare of her hips, to the quickening rise and fall of her breasts, Simon's perusal was slow and thorough, his eyes narrowing fractionally.

"I recognize the dog," he said, squinting down at her playfully, "but are you sure you're the same woman who was here on his behalf yesterday?"

Lucy was quite sure that she ought to take offense, if not at the remark then surely at the frank, compelling insolence of his appraisal, but in the end the warmth in his eyes and the easy, bantering amusement in his tone were hard to resist. "I distinctly remember telling you that I had bad days," she said, smiling up at him sweetly. "Did I neglect to mention that I have good ones as well?"

At that Simon laughed out loud, and to Lucy's ears it was a wonderful sound, deep and rich and melodic.

"So you have, Lucy Whitcomb," he said softly. "So you have."

Unwittingly Lucy's gaze was drawn to his. Their eyes locked in silent communication, and she felt herself being mesmerized by the compelling, sensual invitation she read in his expression. All at once, she found herself wondering what it would be like to move forward into his arms, to press herself against his lean, hard body and to kiss and be kissed by his warm, supple lips. The thought sent a tingle up and down her spine, a deliciously erotic frisson causing her to shiver slightly in anticipation.

Man your battle stations, Lucy thought dazedly.

Her plan was about to begin.

3

It was Simon who broke away first, galvanized into action by the slight tremor that rippled through her body. "You must be cold," he said, pulling his eyes away and, with them, what little warmth Lucy still possessed. For a moment, he looked down at her sternly, and Lucy knew he was about to comment on her attire, or lack thereof, then instead he simply shrugged as if nothing about the way she chose to dress could surprise him anymore. "Come on, let's go inside. I've got some coffee already made."

Simon led the way across the deck, and Lucy found herself following automatically in his wake, like a donkey going after a dangling carrot. "Could you make that tea?" she asked, more out of a need to mask her confusion than because she cared in the slightest what it was that she drank.

"I think I can manage that." Simon's dark eyes glittered with amusement as though he were fully aware

of her discomfiture, but he said nothing. He held open
the back door and ushered her inside, with Duncan
trotting along happily behind.

Lucy realized later that the dwelling's unusual exterior
should have prepared her for the delights she was to find
within. But at the moment, her thoughts were on a
different plane entirely, so that upon entering she was
struck again by the intrinsic beauty of the house's design.
Rather than being divided into rooms, the first floor
consisted of a large open living space, whose divisions
were few and subtly made so that one area flowed into
another according to the dictates of need and function,
the whole a harmonious blend that was uniquely pleasing
to the eye.

A spiral staircase in the corner led up to the second
floor, which circled around three sides of the room
leaving the middle and back areas open to the sky-lighted
ceiling above and the glass wall behind. This arrangement took full advantage of the sun, bathing the interior
of the house in warm, natural light. An enormous stone
fireplace dominated one of the few inner walls, opening
on one side into the living room with its Dhurrie rug and
sleek, white modern furniture; and on the other, into the
kitchen, a room with inlaid tile floors, butcher-block
counters and also, Lucy realized quickly, every conceiv-
able appliance known to man.

"Are you sure this is the kitchen?" she asked lightly,
following him inside. "It looks like Houston Control."

"Don't tell me you're one of those liberated women
who doesn't know how to cook?" Simon said over his
shoulder as he filled a kettle with water and set it down on
the gas burner of the gleaming stove.

"Guilty as charged, I'm afraid," said Lucy. She sat
down in a cane-backed rocking chair by the fireplace,
one of the many eclectic touches in the homey room.
Pushing with her toe, she began to rock slowly back and

forth. "I spent the first twenty-five years of my life thinking that quantity was much more important than quality. I ate anything and everything—from Big Macs to brownies to whole gallons of ice cream. Why go out of your way to prepare food when everything you see tastes good to you?"

"Hmm," Simon said thoughtfully, pouring himself a cup of coffee from the pot on the counter. "I never looked at it quite that way before." Deliberately his glance roamed up and down her body, clinically assessing its size and shape. "If you don't mind my saying so, you must have weighed a ton."

"I did," Lucy admitted, then immediately wished she could recall the words. What in the world was she doing telling him these things? He'd get all the wrong ideas. She wanted him to see her as a svelte siren, not a rehabilitated binger!

Simon cocked an eyebrow in disbelief. "Is that why you run?" The kettle boiled and whistled, and he poured the steaming water into a china teapot, then set it aside to steep.

"That's why I started." Lucy nodded. "I was determined to lose weight and I needed some sort of exercise that was easy, something I could do on my own without any sort of special skills or equipment—you know, something there was absolutely no excuse for not doing, otherwise I knew I'd never do it. But now I run because I enjoy it. I love the peace and the solitude when I'm out by myself so early in the morning. And I love the feeling of invincibility it gives me to know my body's in shape— running like a well-oiled machine with all its parts in the proper order."

"Oh, I'd say your parts were in order all right," Simon agreed, leering down at her cheerfully. He filled a large ceramic mug with tea, then delivered it into her waiting hands. "Lemon? Sugar?"

"Just lemon, please." Deliberately she slanted him a cool, assessing look in what she was sure was a terribly sophisticated fashion. "Off hand, I'd say there's precious little wrong with your form either. What do you do to stay in shape?"

"Tennis in the summer, racquetball in the winter." Simon leaned back casually against the butcher-block counter in the middle of the room. "Want to compare muscles?" he offered with an engagingly hopeful grin. "I'm told I play a mean game of doctor."

The teasing invitation was so unexpected that, in spite of herself, Lucy laughed out loud, forgetting the veneer of jaded sophistication she had meant to maintain and causing the rocker to roll forward with a sudden jolt, which sent several drops of hot tea splashing down onto the front of her dress.

In an instant, Simon was beside her, napkin at the ready. Solicitously he lifted the cup from her hand, then knelt before her to dab at the spots that dotted the bodice of the silk dress. Immediately Lucy flushed with aware-ness, realizing that the clean-up operation, of necessity, entailed fingers brushing lightly back and forth over her breasts. Of their own volition, they swelled beneath his touch as if offering themselves for further attention, and Lucy cringed inwardly with embarrassment. Simon seemed totally oblivious to the turmoil he was causing, bending to the task with all the impersonal efficiency of a mechanic rotating tires. Embarrassment turned to cha-grin then, and Lucy whisked the napkin out of his hand to finish the job herself.

"Do I take it the answer is no?"

"No what?" said Lucy, completely at sea as she looked up from what she was doing to find that his face was startlingly close.

"No muscle contest?" Simon said softly.

He's going to kiss me, she thought. I want him to kiss

me. But he didn't. Instead, he rocked back on his heels and rose to his feet, grasping her hands firmly to pull her up beside him. Now? she wondered hopefully, realizing that the slightest step on her part would fit her quite satisfactorily into his arms. Invitingly, she tilted her face up toward his, but again he stepped away, and Lucy all but swore with frustration. I must be doing something wrong, she thought irritably. But what is it?

"Something the matter?" asked Simon, his tawny brown eyes twinkling merrily.

"Not a thing," Lucy replied coolly, determined not to reveal any more than she already had. Deliberately, she looked down and checked her watch for the time. "Although I'm afraid I must be getting back to work. I've been gone far too long as it is."

"What do you do?" Simon asked curiously. He led the way down a wide hallway to the front door, and Lucy couldn't help being a little disappointed that he'd complied so readily with her decision to leave. Then again, she realized, perhaps it was only courtesy that had prompted him to invite her inside in the first place. For all she knew, that sudden moment of awareness that had passed between them on the deck could be an everyday occurrence for him, nothing out of the ordinary at all. Lucy frowned. For some reason, that thought was profoundly depressing.

"I own a candy store on Main Street called Sweet Tooth," she replied absently as they arrived at the front door.

Simon reached out to grasp the knob but made no move to open the door, instead looking down at her in the hallway's dim light, his expression one of puzzlement. "If you were at work, how did you know that Duncan was over here?"

Lucy shrugged. "He spends the days at the store with me. Usually he's very good, but this morning he bolted out the front door. It didn't take too many guesses to figure out which way he'd go."

"You have a dog living in your candy store? Does the Board of Health know about that?"

"Of course," Lucy lied shamelessly. "He's a very clean dog."

"Clean or not . . ." Simon shook his head in disapproval.

"Oh, for Pete's sake, don't go all pious on me!" Lucy snapped. Her brows drawn downward in a frown, she peered at him closely. "Now that I think about it, you look the type. I'll bet you served as hall monitor in high school, too."

"What type is that?" asked Simon, answering her frown with one of his own.

"Goody two-shoes!"

"Perhaps, like you, I have my good days and my bad days." Simon shrugged.

"Oh?" Lucy cocked an eyebrow. "And which is this?"

"Definitely the latter," said Simon, pretending to take offense. "Can't you tell I've been on my best behavior?"

"What on earth for?" Lucy exploded without stopping to think, then immediately wished she could recall her impetuous words.

"Self-defense," Simon replied with a cheeky grin.

Irritably Lucy planted her palms on her hips. "What is that supposed to mean?" she demanded, pulling herself up to her full height, which, heels and all, was still several inches shorter than his. "Do I look like the man-eating type?"

"You told me yourself that you were a liberated woman," Simon pointed out as though it were the most obvious thing in the world, "and the last time I dared to kiss someone who called herself that, I ended up with a half-hour lecture on the horrors of male domination."

"I never said I wanted to be dominated!" Lucy cried, outraged.

"Then what are you getting so excited about?"

"You know, yesterday I didn't like you," Lucy sputtered angrily, "and today I think I like you even less!"

"Oh well," Simon said with obvious lack of concern. "There's always tomorrow."

"Not for me there isn't!"

"Planning to die tonight?" Simon queried sardonically.

"You know what I mean," Lucy snapped.

"I do," Simon said calmly. "Thousands wouldn't."

"Don't you dare make fun of me!"

"Then don't you take your frustrations out on me," Simon countered.

"I am not frustrated!" Lucy denied quickly.

"Really?" Simon raised one eyebrow delicately. "It seems to me that we were getting along fine until I chose to ignore those signals you were sending out back in the kitchen."

"I don't know what you're talking about," Lucy cried quickly, too quickly.

"This," said Simon, grasping her shoulders and pulling her forward suddenly into his arms, his eyes dark with intent. "This is what I'm talking about."

Taken by surprise, Lucy's instinctive response was to brace her hands against his shoulders and push away, an act that gained her nothing. Simon's arms simply curled more tightly about her waist, holding her still as his mouth descended slowly toward hers. For a brief moment, pride seemed to demand that she resist the embrace on principle's sake, but her senses rebelled at the very idea, all too eager to partake in the festivities.

Giving in, as she had known she would, Lucy melted forward. Her eyelids fluttered shut, and she felt his breath mingling with her own as his lips found hers, lightly at first, and then with growing urgency as the kiss molded them together. His hand traveled down her back to the base of her spine, pressing her against the hard length of his body. Lucy became totally, vibrantly aware of the long, lean thighs molded against her own and of the soft fullness of her breasts as they were crushed against the warm muscles of his chest. A sigh escaped from deep within her throat. Her body seemed to melt beneath the mastery of his touch, and Simon groaned and gathered her closer still, his tongue slipping in between her parted lips to sample the sweetness within. She had been kissed before, but never like this, never with a searing intensity that rocked her to her very core. Her body responded instinctively to Simon's sweet seduction of her senses, turning to liquid fire as his mouth moved over hers, possessing it completely.

My, he's good at this, Lucy thought dreamily, as soft, hot waves of desire washed over her, awakening her to sensations she hadn't even known existed. But, of course, he was supposed to be. After all, wasn't that why she was there? Then conscious thought fled as she became aware of nothing save the throbbing, pulsating needs of her own body and the potent, heady magic of the man who inspired them.

Slowly her head began to spin; she felt as though it were whirling off into the clouds on a voyage all its own. Their tongues teased and tasted, moving in unison to perform a sensual, erotic dance of shared desire. Lucy's hand moved downward to find the front opening of Simon's shirt, trembling over the buttons briefly before slipping inside to caress the warmth of his flesh, her fingers curling themselves in the mat of crisp blond hair she found within. Immediately Simon shuddered in response, a vibration that rippled through her own body as well, enflaming her senses still more.

Then, all too soon, it was over. With incredible tenderness, Simon reached up with both hands to cup the sides of her face, his fingers tangling in the thick russet curls of her hair, his thumbs moving in a sweetly erotic rhythm over her cheeks as he held her head steady and pulled his lips away. With his lids half lowered, he looked down at her through eyes that smoldered black with desire.

"Well?" he said softly.

"Well what?" asked Lucy, still caught up in the powerful spell he had woven around them and not at all anxious for it to end.

"Did you get what you wanted?"

The mocking words brought her back down to earth with a jolt. "No," she lied deliberately, "I got what you wanted."

"Liar!" Simon accused, eyes twinkling with amusement.

"Bully!" Lucy returned with spirit.

All at once in complete accord, they pulled back fractionally and looked each other straight in the eye, then laughed aloud in shared merriment, enormously pleased with themselves.

"I think, Lucy Whitcomb, that I'd like to get to know you better—much better," Simon said thoughtfully when the laughter had died. They continued to stand within the circle of each other's arms. "Will you have dinner with me Saturday night?"

You had to say one thing for these Casanova types, Lucy thought happily, they didn't waste any time. "I'd love to," she said, smiling, making no attempt to mask her delight.

"We'll eat here," said Simon, planning aloud. Then, realizing she might want some say in the matter, he looked down quickly for her consent. "That is, if it's all right with you?"

"That depends," Lucy teased, pretending to consider the offer. "Are you a good cook?"

"Very." Simon's dark eyes crinkled with amusement.

"And modest with it." Lucy grinned. "But are you sure you want to go to all that trouble?" To someone whose idea of cooking was to pop a T.V. dinner into the microwave, the very thought of preparing a real meal suitable for guests seemed like an undertaking roughly comparable to the invasion of Normandy.

"Sure, no problem at all," Simon assured her. "I love to cook, but I hardly ever bother with anything elaborate when I've got only myself to feed. Believe me, it will be a pleasure to get back into the kitchen."

"In that case, you're on," said Lucy, regretfully stepping back out of his warm embrace.

"Seven o'clock?"

"I'll be here."

With equal reluctance, Simon released her, then turned to open the front door. Duncan skittered out behind them, all but forgotten and clearly affronted by that fact. In a bid for attention, he tried unsuccessfully to wedge himself between them as they followed the flagstone walk around the house.

"Don't worry, old man," said Simon, chucking the poodle affectionately under the chin. "She's all yours for the rest of the week, so take good care of her, you hear?"

With minimal fuss, they were installed in the BMW, and as Lucy rolled down her window, Simon leaned into the car and bestowed a light, teasing kiss on the tip of her nose.

"See you Saturday," she said softly, and he nodded, then backed away.

Throwing the car into first, Lucy shot away down the driveway, her spirits in high gear, as a single all-encompassing thought filled her mind: *Whoopee!*

4

By the time Saturday night arrived, Lucy was ready, satisfied that this time nothing had been left to chance. Twice before Simon had managed to catch her at a disadvantage, but tonight she was determined to be nothing less than a vision of loveliness—the picture of cool, poised sophistication.

With that thought in mind, she'd gone shopping on Thursday night when the stores were open late, first visiting Saks, then Lord & Taylor, then finally Bloomingdale's, where she had found exactly what she was after—a dress that would knock Simon Farlow's socks off. It was made of cashmere the same deep cobalt shade of blue as her eyes, the material so soft and supple that it hugged the curves of her figure lovingly; the vee-styled neckline in front plunged just low enough to tantalize without being tasteless. Essentially a sweaterdress, it was elegant, yet not overdone—the perfect choice for a brisk autumn evening in Connecticut.

Now, standing before the full-length mirror on the inside of her closet door, Lucy studied her reflection critically and was pleased with what she saw. Her hair was freshly washed and set, and a vigorous brushing seemed to have endowed the red gold tresses with a life of their own. They curled around her head like a shimmering veil. She had applied dusky rose blusher high on her cheekbones, then used a smoky gray eyeshadow to outline and offset the brilliance of her eyes. A slick of plum-colored gloss on her lips supplied the finishing touch.

All in all not a bad job, she decided, nodding to herself in pleased satisfaction. You'd better be on your toes tonight, Mr. Farlow, because this lady is a force to be reckoned with.

It was exactly seven o'clock when Lucy arrived at Simon's door, a chilled bottle of Pouilly Fuissé clutched beneath her arm. No sooner had she rung the bell, however, than the ebullient feeling of self-confidence that had carried her thus far seemed to disappear entirely. Nervously she licked her lips to moisten them, then reached up to rake her fingers through her hair, not at all encouraged by the sudden realization that the term "fashionably late" had been coined with just such occasions in mind. What if Simon wasn't ready yet? she wondered. What if he thought she was overeager, or even worse, desperate? What if . . .

It was almost a relief to have the door thrown open before her, cutting off the ravings of her overactive imagination before they could go any further. For a moment, Lucy simply stared at Simon wordlessly, basking in the warmth of his smile and more grateful than he would ever know for the glowing welcome she saw in his eyes.

"Come on in," he invited, opening the door wide to

usher her inside. "Your timing is perfect. If there's one thing I love in a woman, it's punctuality."

Startled by his observation, Lucy's head snapped around in surprise, only to find herself staring at Simon's back as he took the coat he had lifted from her shoulders and hung it in the closet by the door. This man had an uncanny knack for reading her mind—a trait no doubt fostered by years of experience in the field, she thought wryly. But it would do to watch her step around him because if she wasn't careful she soon wouldn't have any secrets left at all!

Closing the door, Simon turned to face her once more. He smiled, his tawny brown eyes traveling slowly up and down the length of her body, making no attempt to hide his approval. "Have I told you yet that you look lovely?" he inquired, taking her arm and guiding her down the hall to the spacious living room.

Lucy shook her head. "No, you haven't—but please, feel free to step in and do so at any time."

"You look lovely," Simon repeated unnecessarily, and they both laughed together.

My, what a charmer, thought Lucy, amused, yet at the same time pleased by Simon's blatant flattery. I'll bet he could sweet talk the trunk off an elephant if he put his mind to it.

"So do you," she replied honestly. Looking him up and down, Lucy realized this was the first time she had seen him dressed in anything but denim and flannel. If she had thought him impressive before, it was nothing compared to what he looked like now. His clothes, a pair of smooth-fitting khaki pants, a crisp pin-striped shirt and a yellow, bulky-knit cotton sweater, suited him well, emphasizing the breadth of his shoulders and the well-toned muscles of his physique. He looked very comfortable, very relaxed and, at the same time, sexy as all hell.

The aura of masculinity surrounding him was almost tangible, the seductive power of its attraction reaching out to Lucy's senses in a way that made her toes curl within the soft, Italian leather pumps that encased them.

There was no doubt about it, she decided happily, this man was major league all the way.

"Is that for me, or were you afraid you might need an emergency care package later?" Simon asked with a grin, and Lucy followed the line of his gaze and was chagrined to realize that she was still clutching tightly to the bottle of white wine she had brought as a gift.

"Actually," she retorted, "I was hoping we might drink it together, but if you're that thirsty . . ." Eloquently she shrugged her slim shoulders, trying hard not to smile.

"Are you implying I might not be big enough to share?" Simon demanded, pretending to take offense.

"Not at all. I'm sure *you're* more than enough to go around," Lucy teased, deliberately misunderstanding his meaning, "but it's the distribution of the wine that's got me worried."

"Then put your fears to rest," Simon said expansively. "Your wish is my command." Waving her to the sleek white couch in front of the fireplace, he carried the bottle of wine over to a portable bar in the corner and set about uncorking it.

Left to her own devices, Lucy took a moment to study her surroundings appreciatively. The large room was decorated in shades of ecru and ivory with light blue used as an accent color in the Oriental vases standing on either end of the mantelpiece, in the soft muted watercolors adorning the walls and in the intricate design of the rug beneath her feet. The furnishings were spare, yet not sparse, with a decided lack of clutter. The overall effect was one of low-key simplicity, which prompted the eye to move onward to the real focal point of the room, the great glass wall. If anything, the view was even more impressive at night than during the day. Strategically placed spotlights illuminated the fields and woods of Simon's yard, letting Mother Nature provide the perfect backdrop and bringing all the beauty of the outdoors inside.

Simon had lit a fire in the huge stone fireplace, and the flames leapt and crackled merrily, imparting a feeling of warmth and coziness that belied the room's size. Leaning back comfortably against the cushions of the couch, Lucy let her gaze wander on. It was arrested almost immediately by the sight of a small pile of well-chewed bones lying next to the hearth.

"I hope those belong to Tess," she said lightly as Simon handed her a glass of wine then sat down beside her on the couch.

"Is there any doubt?" Simon's mahogany eyes glittered with amusement.

"Oh, I don't know." Lucy shrugged and said teasingly, "I do seem to remember you said something about dominating people? I thought perhaps those might be the remains of an old girl friend or two . . ."

"Never," Simon growled, his eyes finding hers and holding them. "I like my women alive and kicking, thank you."

"I'll have to remember that," Lucy said softly, shocked and yet at the same time thrilled to discover that the potent magic of his gaze was enough to set her senses tingling with awareness. A creeping sensation of warmth stole throughout her entire body, awakening her to her own potential as a woman in a way that was new and unexplored, yet infinitely compelling in its attraction. Suddenly disconcerted by the strength of these unfamiliar feelings, Lucy tore her eyes away and took a hasty sip of wine.

"You said the other day that you had shipped Tess to Colorado?" she asked, determined to restore their communication to more normal channels. "When will she be back?"

"Early this week," Simon replied easily, as though nothing at all were amiss. "I called to check on her, and she's already been bred. Now they're just waiting for her to go out of season before sending her home."

"You must miss her when she's gone," Lucy remarked, knowing how important Duncan's presence was to her own peace of mind.

"I do." Simon nodded before adding almost sheepishly, "Probably even more than I like to admit. When you live alone, it's amazing how attached you can become to an animal, especially a dog like Tess who gives everything she has and asks for nothing in return."

"I know just what you mean," Lucy agreed. "I've had Duncan for five years, and it's hard for me to imagine what I'd ever do without him." Raising her wine glass to her lips, she looked up slyly from beneath her lowered lashes, knowing full well that she was about to throw down a gauntlet Simon wouldn't be able to resist. "Then again, he is a poodle. And everyone knows they're by far the smartest breed of dog."

"Oh, I don't know," Simon said nonchalantly, but Lucy knew she had his full attention. "Actually, I'm kind of partial to golden retrievers myself."

"When I was little, the family next door owned a golden," she reminisced deliberately, unable to resist baiting him. "Some smart dog he was—always barking his head off or digging holes in our yard."

"That kind of behavior has nothing to do with a dog's intelligence," Simon said sternly. "That's training, or lack of it, pure and simple. I'm a great believer in the idea that all dogs should be worked in obedience. People who don't know how to manage their pets shouldn't have them in the first place." Leaning his arm across the top of the cushions behind them, Simon grinned as he turned to face her. "Don't tell me, let me guess—his name was Goldie, right?"

Nodding, Lucy grinned in return. "How'd you know?"

Simon shook his head in exasperation. "It was inevitable. Sometimes I think nearly half of them must be named that."

"But not yours," Lucy mused aloud. "Tess—it's a pretty name. Does it have any significance?"

"Actually it does. In college I became a great fan of Thomas Hardy, so she was named after one of my favorite characters in literature, Tess of the d'Urbervilles."

"Really," said Lucy, a deliciously wicked smile curving her lips upward. "I named Duncan after one of my favorites as well." Pausing, she sipped her wine slowly, waiting for him to guess.

At the other end of the couch, Simon frowned thoughtfully. Sipping his wine as well, he stalled for time as he mulled over the name, obviously racking his brain for a literary hero named Duncan and unwilling to admit that she had him stumped. Several moments passed before he gave a small, triumphant nod. "I've got it," he announced, hazarding a guess, "the king in *Macbeth?*"

"Nooo," Lucy said slowly, her blue eyes lighting up impishly as she shook her head. "I said it was a favorite of mine, but I didn't say a favorite what. Do you give up?"

Reluctantly Simon nodded.

"Dunkin' Donuts," Lucy informed him smugly, watching the expression of incredulity that flitted across his features briefly, only to be replaced by genuine amusement as he broke up laughing.

"You *are* kidding, aren't you?" Simon demanded when he had caught his breath.

Lucy shook her head. "To tell the truth, I can't take full responsibility for the choice. A friend of mine suggested it, but considering the strength of my allegiance to their products, it seemed like a good idea at the time."

Looking over at her, Simon pursed his lips thoughtful-ly, but his sable eyes glittered with amusement, and Lucy had a sneaking suspicion he was about to get back some of his own. "That's the second time you've mentioned that you love to eat," he pointed out. "I only hope that I've bought enough food!"

"*Loved* to eat," Lucy corrected him firmly. "That part of my life is strictly in the past." For a moment she stared broodingly into the fire. When she finally broke the silence between them, she surprised even herself by admitting, "To tell the truth, I'm not sure I ever really did enjoy eating all that much. It was just something to do—I honestly can't remember ever giving it any thought." Glancing up, she found Simon watching and shrugged self-consciously. "Most people breathe. I ate."

"Were you always heavy?" asked Simon, and Lucy was disconcerted to see that he seemed genuinely inter-ested in her answer.

"From the time I was a small child," she replied slowly, pondering the fact that once again she was telling Simon more than she had meant to, opening herself up to him in a most unfamiliar way. Feeling suddenly defensive, she steered the conversation toward less personal matters. "Actually I've since discovered that the cycle I fell into is a very common one. Think for a moment how often food tends to be doled out as a means of reward and punishment in a child's life. When you're good, your mother gives you a cookie. When you're bad, you get sent to bed without any dinner. It's no wonder that children often come to equate food with love and acceptance."

"Did you?" Simon asked softly, deftly steering the conversation right back.

"I suppose so," Lucy admitted. "But in my case, the problem was heightened by the fact that between my father and my three older brothers, my mother had four men, all over six feet tall, to cook for. They ate everything in sight and, watching them as I grew up, so did I." Pausing, Lucy smiled ruefully. "The difference was that their calories got distributed over substantially larger frames than mine did. In the end, they got big and strong, and all I got was big and fat."

"And then?" Simon prompted gently.

Lucy shrugged. "Then, when I reached the age of twenty-five I decided I'd had enough. There I was in the prime of my life, and yet I had the distinct impression that some of the best things in life were simply passing me by. So I went out and got a diet I could stick to, started running every morning, and . . ." Lucy grinned, holding out her hands to display her body playfully . . . "the rest, as they say, is history."

"Well done, Slim!" Simon returned her grin with one of his own. "I think most historians would agree, few campaigns in history were as successful as yours seems to have been." Rising to his feet, he reached down and pulled her up alongside him. "And speaking of food—if those wonderful smells emanating from the kitchen are anything to go by, I think our dinner must be just about ready."

In no time at all, Lucy had been installed in the cane-backed rocker and instructed to finish her wine while Simon, wielding cooking utensils with the skill of a master, put the finishing touches on the meal. Watching in fascination as he stirred and tossed, sprinkled and tasted, she quickly realized that the dinner he had prepared was to be a veritable feast. If the evidence gathered by her eyes and nose was correct, there was Fettucine Alfredo for the appetizer, followed by a spinach salad, then the main course of Coquilles St. Jacques.

Rocking back and forth in her chair, Lucy groaned inwardly just thinking of the effect all that food was going to have on her diet. The pasta with its rich sauce would be a disaster, even if it did smell out of this world. The salad was not too fattening—she'd watched him dress it lightly. But while the scallops by themselves would have been fine, the wine and cream sauce they swam in was another thing entirely, as were the side dishes of rice pilaf and asparagus smothered in hollandaise.

How could he do such a thing? Lucy wondered indignantly. Why, the whole meal was a dieter's nightmare! Or dream come true, she amended wryly, as her good humor reasserted itself. Oh well, it was only one meal, she decided, mentally throwing up her hands in dismayed resignation. As long as she was going to fall off the wagon, she might as well go whole hog—so to speak.

It wasn't until everything was in readiness on the candlelit table that Lucy realized her expression must have betrayed her thoughts, for as Simon held out her chair he regarded her sternly and said, "No picking at your food now, Slim. I expect you to eat everything on your plate. In fact as the chef, I demand it. After I've slaved over a hot stove all day, the least you can do is be a good guest and be properly appreciative."

Leering down at her figure cheerfully, he added, "Besides, I don't know what you're so worried about. You look fine to me. In fact, you could probably stand to gain a few pounds."

"Shows what you know," Lucy sniffed, glaring up at him.

Undaunted, Simon grinned. "I'll have you know I have an artist's eye for these things."

"If you have then you must have used Rubens for a role model," Lucy said sweetly. "You know, the painter who did all those chubby nudes?"

"Chubby?" Simon growled. "Never! Rubens's women were soft, voluptuous—cuddly."

"They looked like baby hippos."

"Tsk, tsk." Simon shook his head. "Now, Slim—I can

see something's been missing in your appreciation of fine art."

"Oh, I can appreciate those women all right," Lucy shot back, "I just don't want to emulate them, that's all. Now if you don't mind, I think we've discussed my body more than enough for one evening. I don't want to hear another word about it, understand?"

"Yes, ma'am," Simon replied meekly as he pulled out his chair and sat down beside her, but Lucy wasn't fooled at all. She might have won his easy capitulation this time, but she was only deluding herself if she thought for even a moment that she was in charge. When it came to orchestrating relationships, Simon was light years ahead of her, his experience outstripping hers in every direction. He was a master craftsman from whom she could learn, but in all probability, could never hope to better.

Over dinner, Lucy discovered what it was like to feel utterly catered to by a man. Basking in the warmth of his solicitude, she relaxed and gave herself up totally to the pleasures of the moment, glorying in the many facets of Simon's subtle brand of seduction. Their conversation was fast paced and well punctuated with laughter, running the gamut from books to the theater to football. They discovered many views they held in common and several opposing points that produced spirited debate.

One by one, the courses were eaten and cleared away, and by the time they had finished with dessert Lucy knew she had never enjoyed a conversation quite so much, as she met and matched Simon's intellectual thrust and parry with a challenge of her own. Only one brief moment of doubt intruded on what was an otherwise perfect meal, coming toward the end when they were interrupted by the strident ringing of the telephone in the kitchen. Lucy paused midsentence and waited, fully expecting Simon to excuse himself and go answer it. But he only shook his head, bidding her to continue.

"Don't worry," he said as the phone continued to shrill, "after the fifth ring, the machine will pick it up."

"Are you sure you don't want to get it yourself?" she asked uncertainly. "It might be something important."

Slipping his hand across the gleaming expanse of dark wood that separated them, Simon twined his fingers through hers and squeezed gently. "Nothing," he said softly, "could be more important than what I'm doing right now. I'm having a wonderful time talking to a beautiful, sexy and intelligent woman. What more could any man ask?"

Lucy smiled in reply, but inside, her thoughts were uneasy. Did he really think she was so naive she wouldn't recognize a line as outrageous as that? Even for someone as versed in the art of flattery as Simon obviously was, that was laying it on a bit thick. Abruptly Lucy frowned as an unbidden flash of cynicism surfaced, bringing with it the thought that perhaps Simon was able to be the consummate host because he had played this particular scene many times before for a variety of different women. He'd gone out of his way to make her feel special—yet could it be that she was no more than the beneficiary of a skill that practice had made perfect?

Then as quickly as it had come, Lucy pushed the disturbing thought aside. His past simply wasn't any of her business. After all, she had known he was experienced before she'd ever gotten into this. Indeed, it was one of the things that had attracted her to him in the first place. Besides, she was no child—she knew the score. Well, not exactly, Lucy amended hastily, but at least she understood how the game was played. She'd come into this thing with her eyes wide open, prepared to enjoy the moment for what it was, and that was just what she meant to do.

After dinner the dishes were quickly disposed of as Lucy and Simon joined forces in the kitchen to load the dishwasher and do the straightening before retiring together to the living room. All at once, the prospect of what was to come seemed formidable, and Lucy felt possessed by a tremendous urge to keep busy. While Simon bent over the bar once more, filling two small pony glasses with Grand Marnier, she knelt down before the fireplace and drew open the fine mesh curtain to stir up the smoldering ashes with a brass-handled poker. A small pile of wood lay to one side, and she selected two logs to prop atop the andirons, then bolstered them with a handful of dry kindling. Several well-directed puffs of breath fanned the glowing embers until the kindling crackled and caught, and the fire leapt to life once more.

"You're a woman of many talents," Simon said admiringly, and Lucy judged his position to be somewhere directly behind her left ear. "You must have been a girl scout when you were little."

She turned to find that her assessment had been correct; Simon's face was no more than inches away. Still kneeling on the floor, she straightened self-consciously and put more space between them. Breathing room, she thought to herself, drawing a deep, uneven breath. Over Simon's shoulder she saw that from somewhere he had procured a large sheepskin throw, which he had spread out before the hearth.

Nothing like a bachelor pad to provide one with all the comforts, she mused silently—dim lights, a cozy fire, a fine liqueur, and now from out of nowhere, a fur rug. The seduction scene par excellence—in fact, there was only one thing missing.

"What?" she murmured. "No soft music?"

Simon raised one eyebrow fractionally. "Would you like some?" he asked, gesturing toward an elaborate stereo system that filled several shelves of his bookcase. "It's easy to arrange."

"No." Lucy shook her head slowly, taking the glass he

held out to her, then settling down cross-legged on the furry spread. "I don't need any music. It just crossed my mind that it's the only thing missing, that's all."

"Missing?"

Too late, Lucy realized she should never have opened her big mouth. It was obvious to both of them that the entire evening had been orchestrated with precisely this ending in mind. She had known that all along and accepted it, even counted on it. So what right had she now to protest Simon's efficiency at taking them where they both wanted to go?

"Well, you know . . ." she said lamely. "I mean . . . I'm not the only one who must have been a scout. Isn't their motto 'be prepared'?"

Again the eyebrow rose. "Do you object?"

Silently Lucy shook her head, but all at once she was very aware of the opposing impulses warring within her. She felt nervous suddenly, and most unsure. Here she was on the verge of getting what she wanted, yet now that the time was at hand, she couldn't help feeling a small stab of apprehension, just large enough to make her wonder whether she really wanted it at all.

Simon sat down beside her, his long legs tucked beneath him as he set his glass down on the smooth stone of the fireplace, then took hers and put it aside as well. Slowly he reached out to her, his warm, strong fingers settling on her arms just above the elbows and traveling upward to enfold her shoulders with a soft, subtle pressure that urged her forward into his embrace. Anticipating this moment as she had, Lucy gasped at the blazing trail of warmth his fingers seemed to leave in their wake. The temptation to move into his arms was over-powering, but unbelievably, some long dormant instinct chose that moment to assert itself and to Lucy's utter dismay, she found herself stalling for time once more.

"Let's talk about your job," she said brightly, hoping

against hope that he wouldn't notice the thin thread of desperation lacing her voice. "Do you realize we've managed to go this entire evening without once talking about architecture . . ."

Gently but firmly, Simon's hand reached up to trace the curve of her jaw before his fingertips came to rest lightly on her lips, silencing her more effectively than any words would have done. "I've got a better idea," he murmured, his eyes dark with intent, and Lucy knew she didn't need three guesses to figure out what it was. "Let's not talk at all."

It was his tenderness that proved her undoing. As if he sensed her hesitation, Simon slowed his pace to hers, and Lucy shivered slightly but made no effort to move away as his hand slid down the slender column of her throat. His fingers paused there to gather up the thick, heavy strands of a wayward curl, which he tucked away neatly behind her ear in a soft, tantalizing caress. The slow, measured beat of his movements, the way his fingertips traced an intimate pattern over the soft skin of her cheek, unnerved her more than a demanding approach ever could have; when Simon once more urged her forward into his arms, Lucy knew that she could not, would not, resist him.

Carefully, tenderly, he kissed her, his lips brushing back and forth over hers in a series of feather-light caresses as though she were a rare and fragile creature, requiring infinite solicitude. With delicate precision, his lips explored the contours of her face, alighting on her eyelids, her cheeks, the slope of her jaw, before returning to her mouth once more.

It was like falling off a cliff in slow motion, thought Lucy, overcome by a heady, breathless feeling as she fell victim to his soft and subtle persuasion. It was a tease—a tempting, tantalizing tease—calculated to awaken her senses to the possibilities, yet leave them unfulfilled and begging for more. All at once, Lucy felt very sure of what she wanted. Indeed, it seemed as though she had been wanting it for a long time.

Simon pulled back briefly, and her eyelids fluttered open in protest, a soft, questioning moan issuing from deep within her throat. "Don't worry, Slim, I'm not going anywhere," he murmured, and Lucy realized that he was only shifting position, untangling his long legs from beneath him so that he could lie down on the spread. "There now," he said, bringing her down beside him, "isn't that better?"

"Mmm . . . much better," Lucy agreed, her body taking on an almost feline grace as she rolled over onto her back, studying Simon's face above her from beneath a thick fringe of demurely lowered lashes. Mesmerized by his presence so near at hand, she reached upward to stroke the line of his jaw, thrilling to the feel of the strong, hard planes beneath her fingertips.

"In fact there's only one thing wrong," she whispered, her voice husky with desire as she slipped her arms around Simon's neck, then buried her fingers in his burnished, deep golden hair. "You're much too far away."

When his lips descended toward hers as she had known they must, Lucy rose to meet them with a reckless, fiery passion that made Simon groan deeply, then tighten his arms around her in a grip that crushed her to him. The demanding pressure of his kiss drove her lips apart, sweeping her away on a fierce tide of sensation so incredibly sweet that Lucy arched her back upward instinctively, straining toward the source of her pleasure like a flower reaching toward the sun.

Their mouths, their bodies, even their thoughts seemed to be moving in unison as Simon slipped his knee between her thighs. His hands cradling her buttocks, he pressed her to him so that she could feel the power of his growing desire, and Lucy gasped, alight with a glow that started deep within her core and spread to all the reaches of her body, leaving a warm, tingling sensation in its wake.

"Slim?" Simon whispered, pausing for breath.

"Mmm?"

He lay half on top of her, their bodies intertwined, their legs tangled, their faces still so close that even as he spoke she could feel the soft caress of his warm breath upon her cheek. "Do you want to move upstairs?"

Silently Lucy shook her head, not wanting even words to intrude on the magic spell surrounding them. Safe within the warm harbor of Simon's arms, she had never felt so desired, yet at the same time, so protected. No, right that moment, she didn't want to go anywhere—she was sublimely happy right where she was.

Gazing upward, Lucy licked her lips deliberately, drawing her tongue back and forth slowly over their soft pink outline, and Simon watched her as if mesmerized, his deep brown eyes smoldering with the banked fires of his passion. Growing ever surer of herself, Lucy leaned forward, and her tongue continued its quest, flicking gently across his neck till she found the smooth, soft lobe of his ear. Her lips closed over the sensitive skin as she sucked on it gently, and Simon shuddered in response. His hands caressed her lightly from shoulder to thigh, then stopped midway to cup her breast, the soft cashmere no barrier between them at all. Lucy moaned softly, alive with glorious sensation.

The deep vee neckline of the dress allowed Simon the access he sought, and his fingers slipped inside to make short work of the front catch on her bra. Pushing the material away, his hand took its place and the heavy fullness of her breast settled into his waiting palm. Cupping her tenderly, Simon's fingers explored the smooth, silky skin, tracing ever smaller circles around the rosy peak. Impatiently Lucy arched her back, pressing herself forward into the caress as her nipple hardened under his touch and thrust itself into his palm.

"Lean up for me, Slim," Simon murmured, his voice husky with male satisfaction. He shifted his weight slightly so that his hand could slip around behind her neck to the row of tiny pearl buttons that fastened her dress.

Still reeling under the potent magic of his touch, Lucy did not immediately understand the full import of Simon's actions. One by one, his deft fingers tugged the buttons free and, to her dismay, with each passing moment she began to feel a little cooler, and even worse, a little more exposed.

What's the matter with you? she berated herself fiercely. This is what you wanted, isn't it? Well, isn't it? But logic was one thing and emotion was another and, at a time like that, the latter was an easy winner. However unreasonable her fears might be, the very thought of Simon seeing her naked left Lucy swamped with feelings of inadequacy.

"I can't," she whispered, too caught up in her own thoughts to realize that Simon's hands had already gone still as he stared down at her intently. "I just can't."

"Lucy?" Struggling to control his ragged, uneven breathing, Simon grasped her chin between his fingers and turned her face toward his. "What is it?"

"Oh, Simon . . ." Lucy's voice broke on a sob of pure mortification as she realized the unthinkable situation she had gotten herself into—gotten them both into for that matter! So much for sophistication! Simon would be furious with her, and he had every right to be.

"What's the matter?" Simon asked quietly, his voice gentle, yet insistent.

"I can't do this," she whispered raggedly. "Simon, I'm sorry. . . ." Watching his face, Lucy was immediately aware the moment Simon's expression changed, for as she spoke, his features hardened into an ominous frown she did not find reassuring in the least. Uncertainly her voice trailed away, the apology left unfinished.

Simon released her abruptly. Rolling away, he got to his feet, the silence between them all encompassing. He tucked in his shirt and straightened his sweater before extending a hand downward to pull her up, too.

"I know you're angry," Lucy said softly, not knowing where to begin and feeling more inadequate than ever, "and I'm sorry—it was all my fault. I never should have let things go so far . . ."

"Stop right there!" Simon growled.

Lucy did, but something in his tone piqued her curiosity, and she looked up in surprise. Was it her imagination or had Simon actually sounded more disappointed than upset?

"I want you, Slim," he said evenly, "and I'm not about to deny it. But when the time comes for us to make love, it will be right because it's what we both want, not just me and not just you, but both of us, understand?"

Lucy nodded, hope soaring once more. "Then you're not angry?"

Simon swore inelegantly under his breath. Placing both hands on her shoulders, he turned her around so that he could refasten the back of her dress. "I'll tell you what makes me angry," he growled, his hands moving back up the row of buttons with practiced efficiency. "What makes me angry is standing here listening to you apologize for doing what you feel is right." Finishing the task, he turned her back around. His hands continued to grasp her shoulders, and as he gazed down upon her, the look in Simon's eyes was disturbingly warm. "Don't you know that the only person you ever have to please is yourself?"

Whatever reaction Lucy had been expecting, it was certainly not this, and the confusion she felt inside was revealed in her luminous blue eyes as she stared upward in wonder and disbelief.

For a brief moment Simon was still, then abruptly his face was creased by a broad grin. "Come on, Slim," he said, looping an arm around her shoulders and leading her toward the front door. "I think it's about time that you went home—because if you stand there looking at me like that for much longer, I'll be more than a little tempted to forget all my good intentions, and throw you back down on that rug to take up where we left off."

Lucy answered his grin with one of her own, but inside she was more bewildered than ever. The more she knew of Simon, the less it seemed that she knew him at all. One thing, however, was clear. She might have started the evening with a playboy, but she had ended it with a gentleman.

5

The next two weeks seemed to fly by. Lucy was caught up in a flurry of preholiday activity, which she knew from experience would go on through the beginning of January, when there would barely be time to catch her breath before the advent of Valentine's Day and then Easter. Digging up a box of decorations from the back room, she and Margo draped the walls with cardboard skeletons and malevolent-looking black cats, transforming the store's interior into a goblin's delight in honor of Halloween. Their candy selection was geared to the season also, and the counters were stacked high with all the newest novelties: small plastic pumpkins filled with candy corn, pointed witches' caps overflowing with licorice, and the edible wax "disguises" that so delighted the kids—big lips, false teeth, fake moustaches. There was something for everybody's taste, or so Lucy hoped.

As time went on, she was busy behind the scenes as well, checking and rechecking her Christmas orders to be sure all was in readiness. Day by day, shipments of candy canes, barley sugar pops and foil-wrapped chocolate Santas were already beginning to trickle in, filling the small storeroom to capacity until finally she was forced to start stacking boxes in the corner of her office. That inconvenience was small, however, in comparison to the satisfaction Lucy felt at this tangible evidence of her store's success. Judicious promotion and word-of-mouth advertising supplied by delighted shoppers had provided Sweet Tooth with an ever growing clientele; with three big holidays coming up in a row, she knew she would need plenty of stock on hand just to satisfy the large base of steady customers developed over the past two years. Indeed, by all accounts, the next several months held the promise of being her busiest and most profitable ever.

With that in mind, Lucy spent one long afternoon and evening holed up in her office putting together a proposal that was sure to impress even the most tight-fisted loan officer. A statement of her assets and liabilities, her achievements in the past and her plans for the future, it outlined everything she was sure a bank would want to know before extending the larger mortgage she would need in order to expand.

And in the end, because she had done her homework so thoroughly, the meeting with the loan officer was a breeze. Young and genial, the smiling gray-suited banker read through her notes with obvious interest and approval while she sat on the other side of his wide mahogany desk and filled out the application. By the time she left, Lucy had been assured that everything was in order and that her prospects for receiving the mortgage were excellent. Her next stop then was Bonnel Real Estate, where she and Sally Bonnel, the woman who had found Sweet Tooth's present location, sat down over a cup of tea while she outlined her needs.

"You know what kind of building I'm looking for

ideally," said Lucy. "Two large adjoining rooms out front, one for the candy store and the other for the soda parlor. At least two more rooms in back, or above if need be. Clean, bright, airy, big windows, good location. With kitchen facilities already installed if possible, if not I'll have to bring in my own."

Listening to her checklist of requirements, Sally smiled. "But realistically, with prices the way they are in Fairfield County, I also know what you'll settle for—something considerably larger than what you have now, but probably not as nice, sturdy but a little rundown, not quite centrally located but not out in the boonies either. . . ."

"Okay, okay." Lucy laughed. "I get the picture. You know me, I'm not averse to a little handiwork. If it's going to be another fixer-upper, so be it. After all, nobody ever said being a business tycoon was easy!"

"Good." Sally nodded, making copious notes on the pad before her. "As long as you hold that thought, I'm sure we'll be able to find something. I'll start checking around, and let you know when I've lined up a couple of possibilities."

All in all, not a bad day's work, Lucy reflected later that evening. She sat curled up in the corner of her couch with Duncan stretched out asleep beside her, his head resting heavily in her lap. Yes, her life was in pretty good shape right now; although if she wanted to be honest with herself, there was one thing missing. Since that Saturday night two weeks ago when Simon had walked her to her car, kissed her lightly, almost negligently, then watched as she drove off down the driveway, she hadn't heard another word from him.

For the first week, she had been merely puzzled by his silence. By the second, her puzzlement had changed to chagrin.

"So much for all the noble ideals I gave him credit for," Lucy muttered under her breath, reaching out for the mug of low-cal hot chocolate sitting on the table beside her. She was hoping that the sweet, heavy drink would blunt the sharp stab of disappointment that had centered itself in the region of her stomach.

It was time she admitted to herself what had happened, Lucy decided, because the truth of the matter was shockingly clear. Despite the easy rapport they had shared early in the evening, despite the lively conversation and the frequent laughter, in the end it had all come down to the same thing—she hadn't slept with him, and he hadn't called.

"Bum!" she muttered crossly. "Chauvinist! Scalphunter! Two-bit hedonist!" Awakened by the vehemence of her tone, Duncan raised his head, his ears pricked inquisitively.

"Shh, it's all right, I wasn't talking about you," Lucy told the poodle, her voice low and soothing as she tangled her fingers absently in the soft hair of his topknot. "Go back to sleep."

Some great seductress I turned out to be! she mused. Her irritation faded, then gave way to a feeling of reluctant amusement. One date and already I've struck out! Ruefully, Lucy smiled, determined to be philosophical about the whole thing. After all, she wasn't the only one at fault. What kind of Casanova could Simon Farlow be if he wasn't even able to stand up under one small setback? No, she decided, shaking her head. Looking back, it was obvious now that he simply hadn't been the right man for the job.

On Saturdays, Lucy jogged later than usual because Margo came in early to open the shop then left at three, while she rolled in midmorning, then stayed till closing. Nevertheless, the sun had been up for less than an hour the next morning when she climbed out of bed. Shaking the sleep from her eyes, she pulled on her running clothes almost by rote, dressing in a new, black nylon warm-up suit and running shoes.

The temptation of Tess having been removed, Duncan cavorted alongside in his usual place. Lucy made short work of the five-mile run, covering a new route she had adopted just recently, which contained not one, but two sweeps past Simon's house in each circuit.

So what? Lucy told herself defensively. She had every right to run wherever she pleased. She was tired of the old route, she'd been doing it for months. This new one was a much needed change of scenery and nothing more. Still, no matter how much she protested her innocence, her eyes had a telltale way of straying up the long driveway toward the glass and cedar house, giving the game away.

This morning, like all the others during the past two weeks, there was nothing to be seen. And as usual, maintaining her stride without missing a step, Lucy ran on. She had just completed the final loop and was running down the last stretch less than half a mile from home, when she became aware that a sleek silver Porsche had pulled up behind her and was dogging her footsteps faithfully.

Why doesn't he just go on past? she wondered. Granted, there were no sidewalks in this part of New Canaan and she was running along the edge of the road, but surely she wasn't taking up *that* much room?

Then the car drew alongside her, its powerful motor almost idling. The smoked window on the passenger's side was rolled down and a familiar face appeared behind it.

"Hey, lady!" said Simon, grinning broadly as he leaned across the front bucket seats of the car. "Want a lift?"

"Sorry, buddy," Lucy shot back quickly, her tone quite a bit sharper than she'd intended, "but my mother told me never to talk to strangers!"

If he took her retort as a comment on his silence over the last two weeks, Simon showed no sign of it. "That's all right," he assured her genially, "I'm not nearly as strange as you might think."

"Anyone who would offer a jogger a ride must be missing a few screws," Lucy pointed out, her spirits suddenly buoyed by a treacherously unexpected feeling of elation. "After all, the whole point of this is that you do it on your own two feet. That's why it's called running. If you used a car, it would be called something else entirely."

But Simon was undeterred. "So humor me," he said, nudging the sportscar carefully to the side of the road in front of her so that she was forced to come to a halt. "Come on, Slim, hop in. Just looking at you is making me tired."

For a brief moment Lucy resisted, knowing that his high-handed tactics deserved chastising. But he smiled up at her so engagingly, his expression filled with such hope, that she knew she didn't honestly have a prayer of refusing.

Oh well, thought Lucy as she climbed into the car, then helped to wedge Duncan into the small space behind them. There are people in this world who are sane and sensible, and then there are those who willingly take that leap out of the frying pan into the fire. No problem at all figuring out which category she belonged to!

It wasn't until she was settled in the front seat and the car was moving once more that Lucy realized what a sight she must be. Once again, Simon had managed to catch her looking her worst. No wonder he doesn't take me seriously, she thought, grimacing at her reflection in the windshield. At the moment, with her tousled hair and wind-chapped skin, she possessed all the seductive allure of Tugboat Annie!

Determinedly she pulled her eyes away, turning in her seat to face Simon. "You know," she announced, "we've got to stop meeting like this."

Slanting her a look out of the corner of his eye, Simon pretended to be crestfallen. "And here I thought you'd be happy to see me!"

Frowning, Lucy stifled a gasp of indignation. Of all the nerve! Talk about taking somebody for granted!

"Forgive me if I'm wrong," she said evenly, "but aren't you the same gentleman with whom I spent the evening two Saturdays ago?"

"The very same." Simon nodded affably, obviously not about to take the hint.

For a brief moment, there was only silence.

"Well, why the hell haven't you called me?" Lucy blurted out, surprising herself as much as anybody by the question.

For a moment, Simon's eyes left the road and he studied her intently. "Why haven't *you* called *me?*" he asked smoothly.

"But . . . but . . ."

"Yes?" Simon raised one eyebrow expressively.

Because it had never even occurred to her, that was why! Although she certainly wasn't about to tell him that—one of his lectures on women's lib was more than enough, thank you.

"I asked you first," she pointed out, sounding, even to her own ears, lamentably childish.

Glancing over, Simon shrugged. "I've been out on the West Coast for the last ten days on business, and I only got back last night. What's your excuse?"

He'd been away? Lucy thought. He hadn't called because he'd been out of town? What wonderful news! On the other hand, what *was* her excuse? And how on earth had she managed to go from offense to defense so quickly?

"If you've been away all that time, how do you know I haven't called?" she fired back. Nobody ever said this woman couldn't think on her feet!

"The answering machine tells all," Simon revealed, looking over at her reproachfully. "I must admit I was quite disappointed when I arrived home and found you hadn't left any messages. I'd planned to call you later today anyway, but when I saw you run by the house I decided not to wait."

"You came after me?" Lucy gasped, finding this new tidbit of information quite interesting.

"When I see something I want, I go after it," Simon drawled. "So sue me."

"Not me," Lucy replied solemnly, throwing herself into the teasing banter. "Hey, I can understand your impatience. With my sparkling wit, my scintillating conversation and my voluptuous body, I'm quite a package."

"Not to mention your utter lack of clothes sense," Simon pointed out with a grin, "and the way your nose turns a delightful shade of red when you run in the cold morning air."

"What can I say?" Lucy shrugged modestly. "I'm one in a million."

"You'd better be," Simon retorted. "Do you know how many back roads New Canaan has? By the time I got to my car, you'd disappeared. I've been driving around out here looking for you for nearly half an hour!"

"Tsk, tsk, poor thing. That's what impatience will do to you." Lucy shook her head sympathetically, but her blue eyes sparkled. "I guess the least I can do is offer you a cup of coffee for your troubles. If you want to turn left at the next driveway, we've arrived."

"Done," said Simon, pulling in to park the Porsche next to the garage.

Lucy climbed out while Simon pulled his seat forward to free Duncan from the back. Looking at her house as she walked around the car, she saw it suddenly through new eyes and realized how it must appear to Simon—small and entirely ordinary, just a saltbox like so many others, tucked away on its own little half acre lot.

"Nice," Simon commented, nodding his approval, as he followed the line of her gaze.

"Do you really think so?" Lucy asked, feeling unaccountably like an anxious mother at a school play.

"I wouldn't say so if I didn't," Simon said gently. Again he looked over the house, studying it with a practiced eye. "Clean, uncluttered lines, small but totally functional—what more could anybody ask?"

"A back wall made of glass?" Lucy laughed as she led the way to the back door.

Solemnly Simon nodded, pretending to consider the suggestion. "On this house, maybe not. Now if I could interest you in a little gem I know about on Weed Street . . ." Laughingly, his voice trailed away.

"Is that what you do—design and build houses, and then sell them?" Lucy asked curiously. She opened the back door and led the way into the cheery yellow kitchen. "I mean, I know you're an architect, but we never had a chance the other evening to discuss exactly what it is your job entails."

"No, we didn't, did we?" Simon said softly, his sable brown eyes roaming over her slowly, caressingly, before coming back to rest on her parted lips. "As I recall, we found better things to do."

Watching him, Lucy knew exactly what he was thinking, and her first response was one of outrage. Trip or no trip, after two weeks of silence, she was damned if one tender look was going to make her fall into his arms like a ripe tomato!

"Tell me about your work," she said smoothly as though there'd been no break in the conversation at all.

"If you wish," said Simon, backing down with aplomb. He helped himself to a chair beside the small kitchen table as Lucy went to the stove to heat up some water. "In answer to your question, no, I don't build houses or sell them. In the past, I tried forming a partnership with a builder only to find myself getting caught up in the details of construction and sales, which was not what I wanted at all. Design is my forte, it's what I'm good at and what I enjoy, so now I pretty much stick to that."

He paused, and Lucy looked back over her shoulder. "Is instant coffee all right?" At Simon's nod, she pulled two mugs down from the cabinet, measured a spoonful of coffee into one, then tossed a teabag negligently into the other.

"I can see I'm in the presence of a true gourmet," Simon commented, cocking an eyebrow at her slapdash method of preparation. "Just out of curiosity, what would have happened if I'd said no?"

Lucy grinned. "I'd have told you to go elsewhere."

"And a warm, charming hostess, as well." Simon laughed.

"Now wait just a minute!" Lucy cried. "I never advertised any cooking ability. If you're going to go around kidnapping joggers against their will, then I'm afraid you'll just have to take what you get."

"Like I said," Simon conceded, still grinning, "instant will be fine."

"That's what I thought," Lucy said firmly, then turned the conversation back to their earlier topic. "Was your trip to the West Coast successful?"

Leaning back in the chair, his legs propped straight out in front of him, Simon nodded. "I've been commissioned to design a low-income housing complex outside of San Jose, and there were some people there that I needed to see. As a general rule I prefer to work on single-family dwellings—houses that can reflect the personalities of the people who are going to live in and use them. But this sort of project can be fascinating as well. It's a challenge trying to plan housing that will suit the varied needs and desires of a multitude of people, and quite a responsibility, too."

"It sounds as if you love it," said Lucy, setting the steaming cup of coffee down on the table before him, then going back to the counter to retrieve her tea.

"I do." Simon nodded. "I'm very lucky that way. I'm doing a job that I thoroughly enjoy and getting paid to work on top of it." He sipped cautiously at the hot, dark brew, then abruptly set the mug back down on the table with a loud thump and rose to his feet, striding over to join her beside the stove.

"Don't tell me it was that bad?" Lucy asked incredulously, seeing the intent in his dark eyes but not fully understanding its meaning. "Are you planning to murder the chef?"

"Hardly," Simon drawled, taking the cup from her hand and setting it down on the counter behind her. "But it's just occurred to me that there's been a terrible oversight. I have yet to be properly welcomed home from my trip."

"What do you—?"

The rest of the question was lost as Simon towered over her momentarily, then reached out to draw her into his arms.

"Oh!" Lucy gasped, her question answered as, with the first touch of his lips, all her intentions to remain cool and aloof went straight out the window. One ripe tomato, she thought dazedly, coming up.

With an eagerness that refused to be denied, she moved forward into the embrace, sliding her hands up Simon's arms to wind around the back of his neck, her fingers threading through the soft wisps of blond hair at his nape. His mouth covered hers hungrily, his kiss ravenous and insistent. Gone was the tenderness he had shown before. In its place was a fierce, erotic hunger, and Lucy, attuned to the seductive pressure of his hands, his legs, his lips, felt as though no part of her remained untouched by the passionate intensity of his assault.

She sighed deeply, wonderingly, and Simon took full advantage of her parted lips to deepen the kiss, probing and exploring the soft, hidden hollows of her mouth. Then her tongue was moving in time with his, teasing and tempting on a quest of its own. It flicked gently over his lips, which tasted faintly of coffee; then it slid slowly, provocatively into his mouth to trace a tantalizing pattern on the sensitive skin within before withdrawing with deliberate languor to begin the game again.

Simon's answering groan seemed torn from deep within his throat, and Lucy quivered with satisfaction at his response. He cupped her head in the palm of his hand, his fingers tangling in the rich auburn curls as he tilted her head back, arching her body into his and exposing the long, lovely line of her throat, before his mouth swooped down to plunder hers once more.

Vibrantly aware of the lean, hard strength of Simon's body trapping her against the counter, Lucy shuddered as his warm, searching fingers skimmed down the smooth skin of her neck, then lightly over her shoulder. As his hand began its slow, inexorable journey downward, she caught her breath in heady anticipation, willing him to find and cup the breast that had already swelled in anticipation of his touch. With delight, she remembered the feel of his hand caressing her there, the exquisite, exploding sensation of his touch—remembered, and wanted it again.

"Please," she whispered, her voice as soft as a sigh as his fingers settled over the prize he sought.

His lips released hers to murmur something and, her eyes closed, Lucy waited for the sweet, romantic musings that were sure to follow. But to her dismay, Simon lifted his head, and when her eyelids fluttered open she saw that he was staring down at her perplexedly. "What the hell are you wearing?" he demanded. "It feels like a suit of armor!"

For a moment Lucy was utterly baffled, then abruptly she realized what was the matter, and her laughter rang out across the small kitchen, banishing the tender mood that had surrounded them.

"What's so funny?" Simon growled, his tone rife with frustration.

"It's a sport bra," she explained, trying with little success to contain the giggles threatening to erupt all over again. "They're sort of like industrial-strength underwear —I always wear one when I run."

"A sport bra?" Simon muttered, shaking his head disgustedly as if now he had heard everything. "Hasn't anyone ever told you that bras are supposed to be little lacy wisps of nothing that come unhinged at the slightest touch?"

Another male fantasy shattered, Lucy thought, biting down hard on her lower lip to keep from laughing anew at the sight of his thoroughly disgruntled expression.

"Let me give you a bit of advice," she offered, her blue eyes glinting up at him wickedly. "If you want to find wisps of lace underneath, don't start out with a woman who's wearing a sweatsuit and sneakers on top. It decreases your chances dramatically!"

Simon grinned reluctantly, and Lucy stepped back to put some space between them. "What can I tell you?" she said, shrugging apologetically as she looked down at her attire. "This is a very functional outfit—right down to the skin."

"Really?" said Simon, his brown eyes lighting up with

interest as he reached out to pull up her sweatshirt. "This I've got to see!"

"Hey, cut that out!" Lucy cried, pretending to be outraged as she slapped his hands away. She peered up at him, eyes wide with reproach. "And to think you had the nerve to call me frustrated! Maybe I should have had you out there running with me—you know, burning up some of that excess energy?"

Firmly Simon shook his head, his voice rich with innuendo as he said, "If it's energy you want to burn, I can think of much better ways to do it than that."

"I'm sure you can," Lucy replied with a grin, "but I'm afraid thinking is all you're going to be able to do about them at the moment." Over his shoulder, her eyes sought out the time on the large kitchen clock. "Dare I mention that I'm running terribly behind schedule?"

"You can mention it," Simon said affably, "but I'm not sure it will do you any good. Where are you in such a hurry to be off to?"

"Work."

"Work?" Simon echoed, frowning. "But it's Saturday."

"Best day for retail sales," Lucy informed him cheerfully. "Lots of people get cravings on the weekends."

"I can sympathize," Simon drawled, a wicked glint warming his eyes. "I know just how they feel."

"Poor man, I'll have to send you some chocolates," said Lucy, deliberately misunderstanding his meaning. She stepped back and grasped him firmly by the shoulders, then turned him around to face the other way and propelled him in front of her toward the back door.

"Am I being thrown out?" Simon asked conversationally when she opened the door and railroaded him through.

"On your ear, if you like," Lucy offered helpfully.

"No thanks, I'll go under my own power. Never let it

be said that Simon Farlow didn't know how to take a hint, subtle though it may be."

"Now you're getting the right idea." Lucy nodded her approval.

"By the way," said Simon, pausing on the step, "we never did get around to the reason I was going to call you. I've got some court time reserved over at Mead Park tomorrow, and my regular partner's out of town. Would you care to join me?"

"Tennis?" Lucy's voice squeaked her dismay. "You're asking me to play tennis with you?"

"It sure sounds that way." Simon lounged back against the doorjamb, his hands plunged deep into the pockets of his jeans, his eyes watching her intently as if daring her to refuse.

Frowning, Lucy chewed on her lip in frustration. How could she play tennis with him? He was probably every bit as good at that game as he was at everything else, while the closest she'd ever been to a tennis court was watching Wimbledon on TV. In her whole life, she'd never been athletically inclined! The last thing she wanted to do was go out and make a fool of herself, yet, on the other hand, hadn't she spent the last two weeks wanting to see Simon again? Well, here was her chance. But tennis? Her mind screamed in frantic denial. Her?

"I can't," Lucy said slowly, finding no good answer to the dilemma that confronted her. "I don't know how to play."

"No problem." Simon shrugged, disposing of her objection handily. "I'll teach you."

"I don't have a racquet," she pointed out, feeling her feet growing colder by the moment.

"I've got several." Simon grinned, as if waiting to see what she would come up with next.

"No clothes?" She should have known it was a vain attempt before she even tried.

"What you're wearing will be just fine."

"In that case," said Lucy, with a small, nervous laugh, "I'd love to."

"Great. I've reserved time at two o'clock. I'll pick you up at quarter of?"

At Lucy's nod, he straightened up and strode jauntily across the driveway to the Porsche, whistling under his breath as he went.

Of their own volition, her eyes followed him, appreciating the rounded curve of his buttocks, the taut, muscular strength of his thighs and the smooth, molded fit of the jeans that encased them both.

Agreeing to play tennis with Simon wasn't the smartest thing she had ever done. Then again, it might not be the dumbest either, Lucy mused with a reckless grin. After all, Duncan wasn't the only one who was susceptible to Mother Nature's charms. No doubt about it, the call of the wild was a powerful thing.

6

By three o'clock the following afternoon, Lucy knew that she had never regretted anything as much as she was coming to regret the wayward impulse that had brought her to the Mead Park clay courts for an afternoon of tennis with Simon.

Looking back, she decided the day had begun well enough. She had taken Simon at his word, dressing once again in a warm-up suit. This one was a distinct notch above most of her others, having been fashioned out of rich, cream-colored velour with deep burgundy piping for contrast. A pair of sneakers that hadn't seen active duty since college and two pairs of thick white sweat socks completed the outfit—hardly alluring by anybody's standards. To compensate, Lucy had taken special care with her hair and makeup, brushing back the glossy russet curls and holding them in place with a pretty headband. Then she shaded her eyes, her cheeks and her lips with muted, earth-tone colors, putting on just enough so that her features took on an added definition and sparkle, yet still looked entirely natural. She was amply rewarded for her extra efforts by the appreciative gleam in Simon's tawny brown eyes when she met him at the door promptly at one forty-five.

But after that auspicious beginning, the day went straight downhill. To begin with, it was freezing. The weather, which for the past week had treated them to mild Indian summer temperatures in the seventies, had suddenly and without warning dropped overnight. Now the thermometer hovered in the low fifties, while the sun had disappeared behind a bank of clouds, drifting in and out at odd moments, but never managing to provide anything useful in the way of warmth.

Even knowing all this beforehand, Lucy had kept the layers beneath her warm-up suit to a minimum so that her mobility would not be restricted. Leaving the house, she'd been sorely tempted to slip on a down vest, but pride prevented her from making the move. Simon already thought she didn't know how to dress, and she had no desire to confirm his opinion. It was bad enough that she wasn't going to be able to play this game with any flair, or style, or even ability—the least she could do under the circumstances was to try to look the part.

And so she did, Lucy thought crossly. Looked great—felt miserable. He must be part polar bear, she decided, looking over the net to where Simon stood, racquet in hand, patiently feeding shots to her forehand side. Already he had discarded his jacket, stripping down to the smooth-fitting white polo shirt he'd worn underneath, and it seemed only a matter of time until his pants followed. Obviously the cold wasn't bothering him at all. He kept warm by dashing around the court after her erratic returns, his boundless energy and unflagging enthusiasm enough to make Lucy sick.

"Isn't our hour up yet?" she asked wearily. God, it seemed like they'd been out there batting that ball around for ages!

Simon looked down quickly to read his watch. "Almost," he said, grinning happily, "but when I checked in, they told me that no one has reserved the time slot after ours, so we can play right on through if we like."

Hastily Lucy stifled a groan. "Why on earth would we want to do a thing like that?" she muttered under her breath, then made the effort to summon a pale approximation of a smile as she faced him across the court.

Despite Simon's efforts over the past hour, Lucy had managed to learn only one thing so far—that she despised the game of tennis with a passion. Never before had she felt so clumsy, so ungainly, so utterly uncoordinated! If her cheeks hadn't already been so pink from the cold, Lucy knew they would have been flushed with embarrassment. No matter how hard she tried, the racquet remained unwieldy, the ball elusive and her feet pointed stubbornly in the wrong direction.

"Come on, Slim," Simon called encouragingly as he fed her another ball from the seemingly endless supply in the basket by his side. "You can do it. I know you can."

"Oh yeah?" Lucy retorted. Feet planted squarely apart, she propped both hands on her hips, then watched in aggravation as yet another ball went sailing past her shoulder. "I wouldn't be too sure of that if I were you. I'll have you know that when I was little, I had one of those wooden paddles you buy in the dime store—you know, the ones that have a little orange ball hanging at the end of an elastic string? I could never manage to hit that ball either, and those two things were attached to each other, so I don't know what makes you think I have a prayer of mastering this!"

"Tsk, tsk, tsk." Simon shook his head, grinning at her across the net. "Don't take such a defeatist attitude.

93

Don't you know that the key to a good game is all in your head?"

"My head is fine, thank you," Lucy growled irritably. "It's my feet and my arm and *your* racquet that are giving me trouble."

"Okay, one more time," Simon said patiently. "I want you to turn to the side, your shoulder, not your chest, facing the net. Bend your knees, and for God's sake, keep your eye on the ball."

Her brow furrowed in concentration, Lucy did exactly as he said. She swung through and made contact, and everything seemed to be going fine until the ball sailed up over the fence and landed in the court next door.

"You're tilting your racquet head upward. I told you to keep it flat," Simon said grimly, and Lucy realized that his exasperation was finally beginning to mirror her own. "Where is your hand-eye coordination?" he demanded as if such a deficiency was unthinkable. "Didn't you play any sports at all when you were little?"

Glowering back at him, Lucy shook her head. "You must have been young once. I'm sure you remember how it goes—the fat kids are always the last ones to get picked in any game. Usually, they just let me keep score. Besides," she announced, embarrassment and chagrin finally giving way to anger, "I don't know why you keep insisting that I ought to be able to do this. The ability to play tennis is a talent, not an inalienable right!"

"Slim," Simon said softly, walking up to the net, "stop shouting at me."

"I'm not!" Lucy yelled, tossing her racquet down on the ground in disgust.

"And stop feeling sorry for yourself, too."

"I'm not doing that either!"

"No?" Simon raised one eyebrow expressively.

"No," Lucy mumbled, but her voice lacked conviction,

and she bent down and picked up her racquet, dusting the clay off its handle apologetically.

"That's better," said Simon, and the condescending quality in his tone set Lucy off all over again.

"Than what?" she demanded, eyes flashing dangerously.

"I'll take the Fifth on that one," Simon said with a grin that only added fuel to her fire.

"Don't you dare patronize me," Lucy warned. "It's not my fault that you're a coordinated person, and I'm not."

"Nonsense," Simon scoffed. "Everyone has some ability. Your only problem is that you hid behind your fat all those years. Now that excuse is gone, and you still don't want to push yourself, so you're looking for another way out."

"That's not true!" Lucy denied vehemently.

"Oh no?" asked Simon, his anger rising to match her own. "I don't know how else you'd explain what's going on out here. Ever since we arrived, you've had this idea that you can't play tennis, that it's too hard. Hell, I can see from here that you're not even trying. You're afraid to put forth too much effort because you don't want to wind up looking like a fool. Well, look all around you," Simon growled, swinging his racquet in a wide arc. "Look at all these people playing tennis. Some of them are good, and some are not so good, but at least they're all having fun, which is more than I can say for you."

Got it in one, buster, Lucy thought grimly, glaring at him across the net. That was one charge she certainly couldn't refute!

"Then again," Simon added tauntingly, "maybe it's not your fault. Perhaps the wind is a little too strong?" Deliberately, he licked the tip of one finger, holding it up to check the nonexistent breeze. "Or is the sun in your eyes? No? Then maybe it's the surface—does your end need sweeping?"

Scowling angrily, Lucy stalked to the middle of the court where Simon stood, one hand resting on the net separating them. Deliberately she tucked her racquet away beneath one arm, leaving both hands free as she reached up to grasp Simon's collar and jerk it forcibly downward.

"If I were a man," she announced when they stood eye to eye, "I'd punch you right in the nose."

"If you were a man," Simon growled, "I'd have punched you a long time ago."

"Good," Lucy said forcibly. "Just so we understand each other."

Releasing him, she stepped back, discovering as she did so that her anger, having been aired, was rapidly dissipating. In spite of herself, her lips began to twitch at the absurdity of the whole situation. They must look pretty ridiculous after all—two full-grown adults fighting over something as inconsequential as a silly game of tennis. Whoever would have thought he'd be the type to take a stupid game so seriously? Lucy mused, pursing her lips thoughtfully. So Simon thought she was too inhibited to loosen up and have fun, did he? Well, she'd show him!

"Now then," she said, stooping down to pick up the balls at her feet and placing them atop his racquet, "are you planning to stand there all day or did you come here to play tennis?"

Simon's gaze narrowed speculatively as he contemplated her sudden change of mood, but he said nothing as he walked back and once more took up his position on the baseline. For the next fifteen minutes, they managed to achieve a state of peace, if not of total equanimity, as Lucy changed her tactics, deciding to think of the game as a form of jogging with a little arm movement thrown in. Much to her surprise, once she started moving, the play did improve. Not only did she finally warm up, but she was also able to hit the ball better as well.

Never one to stay angry for long, Lucy found that today was no exception. Simon seemed to be giving this thing his best shot, so why shouldn't she? He wanted to see her have fun, and that was exactly what she was going to do! Casting her inhibitions to the wind, Lucy threw herself into the game with abandon. Graceful leaps and energetic bounds carried her from one end of the court to the other. Exaggerating her swing, she turned her forehand into a broad, looping motion, whose momentum twirled her in a small circle more than once. It was on just such an occasion that détente blew up in her face, and the hostilities resumed.

"Lu-cy!" Simon said, his voice laced with exasperation as he caught the ball she had hit back to him, effectively stopping the play. "Just what do you think you're doing?"

Regaining a proper tennis stance somewhat dizzily, she peered at him over the net, her blue eyes round with innocence. "Why, I'm having fun, just like you wanted me to."

The sound that issued back from the other end of the court was part groan and part growl—neither sounded promising, so Lucy decided to ignore it altogether. Absently she poked her index finger through the open throat of her racquet, spinning it end over end like a baton as she waited for his shot.

His features set in a stony frown of disapproval, Simon fed her another ball, this one harder and deeper than those he had hit earlier. With her racquet so far out of position, Lucy hadn't even a prayer of hitting it. Instead she didn't even try, watching the ball fly past with a loud sigh of resignation.

Across the net, Simon scowled. "Would you be serious!"

"Who, me?" cried Lucy, her eyebrows raised in surprise. "Why, I'm perfectly serious. After all, who wouldn't be—standing around outside on a fifty-degree day, chasing after a fuzzy little ball with a weapon the size of a snowshoe? Why, anyone can see just by looking that this is serious stuff."

"Lucy . . ." Simon muttered warningly.

Racquet in hand, she approached the net once more. "Come on, Simon," she said brightly. "Lighten up, would you? War and famine, now they're serious. Rising unemployment and runaway inflation are serious. Tennis is only a game. A game, Simon, do you hear me?"

"I hear you," Simon muttered. Turning his back, he began to gather up the balls littering his end of the court.

"What are you doing?" asked Lucy, truly puzzled as he finished cleaning up his end, then walked around the net to start on hers.

"The game's over," Simon informed her harshly. "It's time to go home."

"But why?" Lucy began to feel like a preschool child tagging along at her mother's heels as she followed Simon around the court, watching him methodically replace the balls in the basket one by one. He was angry, she realized suddenly, really and truly angry, and she hadn't the slightest idea why.

What right did he have to be upset anyway? she wondered indignantly. After all, she was the one who had spent the whole afternoon trying to humor him! He had wanted her to play tennis, and she had. He wanted her to have fun, and she'd managed to do that, too. So why was he now storming around the court in self-righteous outrage?

"Simon?" she said, genuinely bewildered by his behavior. "What's the matter?"

He didn't answer right away, and Lucy waited while he retrieved the last of the balls, then walked over to the bench beside the court and picked up his racquet cover. For a moment she thought that he wasn't going to answer at all. Worse yet, that he was going to continue ignoring her as if she didn't even exist. But when the black plastic cover had been slipped on and zipped into place, and the racquet laid carefully down on the bench beside the basket of balls, Simon turned back around to face her. His voice, when he finally spoke, was ominously low and quiet.

"I'll tell you what's the matter," he said, speaking slowly and distinctly as if he wanted to make sure that she understood every word. "There is a big difference between having fun and making fun, and you know it. Everything is a game with you. You refuse to take anything seriously, including me, or yourself."

"Why should I?" Lucy demanded, utterly baffled by this sudden outburst. What business was it of his how she chose to live her life? If she had learned one thing during her first twenty-five years, it was that it didn't pay to take yourself too seriously, because as soon as you did, someone would be more than willing to burst your bubble. No, it was much better to laugh away the jibes and the barbs—to laugh and pretend that they didn't matter—because sometimes if you tried hard enough and laughed long enough, you could almost believe that they didn't.

"Life is not a joke, Lucy," Simon said forcibly, his thoughts mirroring hers with eerie precision. "It's time that you stopped thinking about what you can't do and started thinking about what you can. You're not that fat little kid anymore, and the sooner you grow up and realize that, the better!"

Stunned into silence by the vehemence of his attack, Lucy was unable to think of a single thing to say. Fuming, she snatched up her own racquet cover and busied herself with slipping it into place, watching surreptitiously out of the corner of her eye as Simon picked up his jacket and shrugged it on.

"Ready?" he asked tersely, and she nodded.

The trip home was accomplished quickly and in silence, not another word being spoken until the silver Porsche pulled up in front of her door only minutes later.

"Don't bother," Lucy snapped as Simon reached for the key to turn off the ignition. "I'll find my own way in." Scrambling inelegantly out of the low car, she succumbed to the childish, but greatly satisfying urge to slam the door behind her. No sooner had she stepped clear than the Porsche backed down the driveway and roared away. "Good riddance to you, too," she muttered under her breath.

Turning to the house, she threw open the back door with a vengeance, only to be confronted by her big black poodle, his tail wagging a deliriously happy welcome. "What's got you in such a good mood?" she said crossly, slamming the door behind her. "Can't you see this is a miserable day?"

Obviously, the poodle couldn't. With a low whine of delight, he jumped up into the air, propping his paws on her chest as his tongue lapped enthusiastically at her face. "Oh, get down, would you?" Lucy growled, pushing the dog away none too gently. "And while you're at it, shut up too."

Finally Duncan seemed to have gotten the message, and his reaction to her rude rebuff was pitiful enough to draw sympathy from even the hardest heart. Immediately he dropped to all fours, his liquid brown eyes open wide with reproach. Then, head and tail drooping, he slunk away to the corner of the kitchen and lay down.

Watching him, Lucy sighed in exasperation. Males! Where did they all get off thinking they had a right to comment, verbally or otherwise, on her behavior? Then, pierced by a small stab of guilt, she relented. Perhaps this one did—after all, they had been friends for a long time.

"All right, I'm sorry," she muttered, dropping to her knees on the floor and welcoming the poodle into her arms. "There now, do you feel better?"

Tail wagging once more, Duncan watched with avid interest as she rose and opened the cupboard over the stove to fish out a handful of dog biscuits. Politely the poodle whisked them out of her hand, then lay back down in the corner to enjoy his treat.

"If only Simon was so easy to get around," Lucy mused aloud, and Duncan obligingly pricked an ear to listen.

Who did he think he was anyway, analyzing her like some smalltime Sigmund Freud! Of all the unmitigated gall! After all, the man was far from blameless himself—why his reputation with the ladies would have done a dozen men proud! But did she go around criticizing his behavior? Nooo, thought Lucy, shaking her head in self-righteous indignation. She kept her nose to herself, right where it belonged. And from now on, Mr. Simon Farlow could do the same!

It wasn't until much later that night as she lay in bed, snuggled under her down comforter and waiting for the blissful oblivion of sleep, which refused to come, that Lucy was finally able to sort through her feelings calmly and rationally, and come to terms with what had happened. In her mind, she replayed the scene on the tennis court, examining this time not only Simon's behavior, but also her own. As her anger over the incident slowly ebbed, her objectivity returned, and Lucy was able to see with a clarity of mind she had not possessed earlier that Simon had indeed had just cause to complain.

Standing out there on the tennis court, engaged in an activity at which she was hopelessly inept, she'd been swamped by insecurity. Rather than admitting her fears, and trying to deal with them like a mature adult, Lucy had taken the easy way out. She had told herself at the time that she was giving Simon what he wanted, but now she could see that that wasn't true at all. No, it wasn't his needs she'd responded to, but her own. Automatically, without even realizing what she was doing, she had slipped back into the pattern of her youth—she had assumed the role of the jolly fat girl and played it to the hilt. Sure that Simon was going to laugh at her, she had quickly moved to give him something nonthreatening, nonhurtful to laugh about. It was a lesson she had learned well as a child and perfected over the ensuing years—the best way to keep people from laughing at her was to ensure that they laughed with her.

Only Simon hadn't been laughing, thought Lucy, and looking back now, she could see why. That realization, however, didn't make her feel any better. Indeed, if anything, she felt worse and, perversely, angrier at him than ever. What right did he have to go messing around inside her head anyway? This was supposed to be an affair of the flesh, not a meeting of the minds. How she elected to live her life was simply none of his damn business!

Predictably, the sleepless night took its toll, as Margo was only too pleased to tell her the following morning when their cars arrived in the parking lot at the same time and they met at the back door to the shop.

"You look awful," Margo informed her cheerfully, leaning closer to peer at the dark shadows beneath Lucy's eyes. "And here I thought things were bad when Simon didn't call. I hate to say it, Luce, but now that loverboy's back in the picture, you look worse than ever."

Lucy's lack of response didn't have the quelling effect she might have hoped for.

"Then again," Margo added, undaunted, "with Simon around, I guess you've got better ways to spend your nights than sleeping."

Feeling tired and cross, Lucy was in no shape to field her assistant's innuendos, and she looked pointedly down her nose at Margo as she fished through her purse for the key, then unlocked the door and let them both inside. "Actually, if you want to know, Simon isn't around," she said shortly, "not since yesterday afternoon, to be exact."

"Uh oh." Margo groaned. "Don't tell me you had a fight with him?"

"All right." Lucy shrugged. "I won't."

Walking down the corridor to the front room, Margo sighed dramatically and flipped on the light switch, illuminating the shop. "You must be crazy," she said, shaking her head in disbelief. "How could any woman in her right mind fight with such a hunk?"

Walking around behind the counter to unlock the cash register, Lucy shot her friend a withering glance. "It's easy," she announced. "Just let him try practicing his curbside psychoanalysis on you someday, and see how long you last."

"Not a case of cerebral concord, I take it?" Margo observed drily.

"Nor physical either," Lucy shot back, her resentment at Simon's highhanded treatment once more coming to the fore.

"You're kidding!" Margo arched an eyebrow, her expression clearly indicating her view that surely this was one area where the man could do no wrong.

"It's not what you think," Lucy said irritably. Ducking down beneath the counter, she found a new roll of tape for the cash register and pulled out a dustcloth at the same time. "We played tennis."

"I didn't know you knew how." Reaching out with one

hand, Margo snagged the cloth Lucy tossed across the room.

"I don't," Lucy muttered as she unwound the end of the tape. "I didn't have the faintest idea how to play when we started, and when we finished nothing had changed. In fact, the only thing I learned in all that time is that Simon Farlow is an arrogant, overbearing, son of a—"

"So what else is new?" Margo interrupted with a careless shrug. "You knew all that when you got yourself into this. Besides, I don't see what difference a few aberrant personality traits make. You told me yourself that it's his body, not his mind, that you're interested in, remember?"

Standing behind the counter, Lucy scowled darkly, convincing her assistant that now was a good time to put the dustcloth to work. Still, she couldn't resist one last parting shot. "I told you this romance business was tricky stuff," she said smugly. "Why, the issue of sex alone has been known to trip up greater minds than ours."

"Wait just a minute!" Lucy cried, looking up from the cash register. "You've got things all wrong. In the first place, Simon and I are not romantically involved. And in the second, we're not even . . ."

"Yes?" Margo prompted curiously.

"We're not . . . I mean, we haven't . . . well, you know what I mean," Lucy finished lamely.

"All right, Luce, if that's the way you want to play it," Margo said in a hurt tone of voice. "Although I thought we were better friends than that. After all, didn't I tell you what went on after Charlie Osgood's clambake? And who was the one who warned you, from dire experience I might add, never to take a ride in Randy Bennet's dinghy?" Deliberately she stuck out her lower lip in a pout. "But if you don't want to discuss Simon Farlow with me, you don't have to."

Taking the performance for the wonderful act it was, Lucy smiled. "I tell you," she insisted, "there's nothing to discuss. Simon and I haven't even gone beyond the kissing stage yet."

Across the room, Margo looked up from her dusting to stare at her friend incredulously. "After all this time? Girl, I've heard of slow starters in my day, but you take the cake!"

The choice retort Lucy was shaping in her mind never got any further. Their conversation was interrupted by the sound of someone pounding on the front door to the shop.

"What the hell?" Lucy muttered irreverently, still bent over the cash register and now more tangled in its tape than ever.

"Oops." Margo giggled. "I forgot to unlatch the door. No wonder we haven't had any customers!"

The man waiting outside to gain admittance was not a customer, however, but rather a delivery man, clutching a small, elegantly wrapped package tied with a large red bow. "Lucy Whitcomb?" he asked, holding out the clipboard for her signature.

"Over there." Margo jerked her thumb over her shoulder. Following the man to the counter, she took over the task of wrestling with the cash register while Lucy signed for the delivery. "What is that?" Margo asked curiously when the man had gone and the box had been laid down atop the glass counter.

"I don't know." Lucy shrugged, genuinely baffled. She picked up the package and turned it over, looking at it from all angles. "There doesn't seem to be a card either."

"Maybe it's inside," Margo offered helpfully. "Come on, don't just stand there. Open it up."

"Hold your horses." Lucy laughed, slipping off the beautiful bow and laying it carefully aside, before tugging at the taped ends that held the wrapping paper in place. "I'm just as curious about this thing as you are."

The trim white box beneath the paper offered no clues either, and Lucy hesitated only a moment before lifting off the lid. There, nestled atop mounds of tissue paper, lay a small white card. Picking it up, she read softly:

"I'm sorry about yesterday. Will you accept my apology and a peace offering to go with it? Just a little something to help you flaunt your assets. It's much more fun than hiding behind your inadequacies, believe me."

Well, at least one question had been answered, Lucy thought, her emotions mixed as she placed the card down on the counter. Reaching into the box, she smoothed aside the paper, wondering what Simon could possibly have sent. She didn't realize that she had been holding her breath until it escaped suddenly in one long whoosh. "Oh, my God!" she exclaimed, her cheeks flushing a brilliant shade of crimson.

As Margo watched with great interest over her shoulder, Lucy lifted out the contents of the box. Using just the tips of her fingers, she held up two lace-trimmed satin bras, one in a creamy shade of champagne beige, the other, a wickedly evocative black.

Behind her, Margo burst out into a fit of giggles that Lucy knew should have been the last straw. She was angry with Simon, after all. She wanted to stay angry with him. But somehow, she just couldn't. The situation was simply too funny, especially when she remembered his all too evident frustration when he had come up against the protective barrier of her sport bra. Obviously Simon had decided that she couldn't be trusted to dress herself properly and had elected to take matters into his own hands!

She could just picture the scene now—that tall, strapping hunk of a man sorting through the dainty underthings in a women's lingerie shop. . . . Abruptly her own laughter erupted as well. The two women fought simultaneously for control, succeeded, then made the mistake of looking each other in the eye and broke up all over again.

"I take back everything I said," Margo choked out several minutes later. "Maybe there's some truth to that old saying after all—you know, slow and steady wins the race?"

"I can't believe he would do such a thing." Lucy gasped breathlessly, reaching up to wipe away the tears of merriment that were streaming down her cheeks.

"I'll say one thing for our Mr. Farlow," said Margo. "He certainly isn't shy." Picking up the bras from where Lucy had dropped them back into the box, she flipped one inside out and showed the label to her boss. "How'd he do for size?"

For some reason, the purely practical question had the effect of setting off Lucy's giggles anew. "Perfect," she replied when she was finally able to speak. "He must have a very refined sense of touch."

"What did I tell you?" Margo nodded wisely. "It pays to deal with men of experience." She paused, then added thoughtfully, "And speaking of dealing with him, are you going to accept?"

"The gift?" Lucy asked, looking up in surprise. Somehow the question had never even occurred to her.

"No silly, the apology," said Margo. "Of course you're going to accept the gift, but the apology is another matter entirely. If he's gone this far, you know he must feel pretty bad. Maybe you ought to let things ride for a while until he's really had a chance to squirm." Margo shrugged airily. "It's not good to make things too easy for a man, you know. A little playing hard to get never hurt anybody's chances."

"Don't be ridiculous," Lucy replied. "Why on earth would I want to make Simon squirm? If the truth be known, we both have something to apologize for after yesterday, and I'm going to call him right this minute and tell him so."

But to Lucy's disgust, she quickly found that it was easier said than done. Sitting down at her desk, she dialed his home phone number, only to be delegated after the fifth ring to the services of the answering machine. Frowning thoughtfully into the receiver, she hung up before the sound of the tone. If ever there was a message that needed a personal touch, surely this was it.

It took only a moment for the gears to click in her mind, and she came up with the name of the Manhattan firm with which Simon was associated. A quick call there, however, proved no more successful than her first attempt had been. Instead she only garnered the unwelcome news that he was once again on the West Coast and was not expected back until the end of the week.

Replacing the receiver in its cradle, Lucy stared off into space broodingly. So he was gone again, she mused, well no matter. She'd catch up with him when he came back. After all, it was only fair. She owed him one.

7

~~~~~~~~~~~~~~

Lucy spent the rest of the week making plans, and by the time she finally managed to reach Simon late Friday night, she was ready. He had made the first move toward closing the breach between them, now it was her turn to reciprocate. Delighting in the sound of his deep, resonant voice, she'd thanked him for his present, then offered to make some amends of her own by cooking dinner for him the following evening, an invitation he'd accepted eagerly.

Planning the scene down to the last detail, Lucy envisioned a cozy dinner for two, an intimate tête-à-tête where they could talk and relax and let bygones be bygones; a perfectly orchestrated evening that would go a long way toward reestablishing the easy rapport they'd once shared. With Margo's help and encouragement, she had mapped out a menu that would be, if not sumptuous, at least fit for company. Bearing in mind her limited culinary skills, they had decided that simplicity was the key. Lucy, who knew six different ways to buy fried chicken in a box but couldn't tell an artichoke from an avocado, had deferred to her assistant's judgment and been told that she was going to broil a couple of filet mignons—a foolproof meal, or so she'd been repeatedly assured.

"It's easy," Margo claimed, whose expertise was the result of a good relationship with her mother's cook. "Chapter one in the cookbook. Any child with an oven and a watch could do it."

Saturday morning, Lucy cleaned the house from stem to stern, then drove down to the market for some last-minute shopping. Margo had backed up her claim by drawing up a detailed list, a step-by-step analysis of the preparations, which boosted Lucy's confidence enormously. From the look of things, she didn't really need any cooking skills at all—just the ability to read and follow directions. Nevertheless, she took no chances, checking and rechecking the list to make sure that no item, however small, was overlooked.

By late afternoon, Lucy's kitchen was a study in controlled chaos. As per the instructions, which were now taped to the side of the refrigerator, she had lettuce in the sink, soaking; cheese on the counter, warming; cheesecake in the icebox, chilling; red wine in a carafe, breathing. The steaks had been marinated, the mushrooms decapitated and the potatoes wrapped in foil ready to be baked.

Honestly! Whoever would have thought that having a nice, simple affair would turn out to be so much trouble? thought Lucy, surveying this scene of domestic bliss with a decidedly skeptical eye. From the start, she had blithely assumed that Simon would be a willing, if not eager, participant in her education; yet here she was, wooing and pursuing with the best of them. Not to mention trying to cook a decent meal for the first time in all her twenty-six years. She had to say one thing for the man, he certainly affected her in strange ways!

Even a long, leisurely bath, which soaked up the better part of an hour, did not prevent her from being ready with plenty of time to spare. Dressed in a pair of fitted, burgundy velvet trousers and a flowing white silk blouse, Lucy knew she looked good. The epitome of elegant sophistication if ever there was one, she thought smugly, checking her image in the mirror's reflection. She looked cool, calm and poised. So what if beneath that brave exterior she was a seething mass of nerves? Nobody, least of all Simon, need ever know.

By the time he arrived, preparations for the meal were progressing quite smoothly. Proceeding on down Margo's list, Lucy had set out the cheese and crackers, made the salad and popped the potatoes into the lower oven. All that remained now was a quick sauté of the mushrooms, an even quicker broiling of the two steaks and presto! all would be done. Julia Child, she thought, eat your heart out!

She had fully expected that there would be an initial awkwardness between them—lingering aftershocks of the previous week's volcano. But when she threw open the door in response to Simon's knock and was immediately folded into a powerful bear hug as he lifted her up and twirled her around on the step, Lucy knew everything was going to be all right.

"God, it's good to see you again!" he said, grinning broadly. Grasping her by the shoulders, he held her out at arm's length and studied her from head to toe as if it had been years, rather than days, since they had seen each other last. "Beautiful," he murmured appreciatively, shaking his head as though in wonder of it all. Releasing her, he shrugged out of his coat and the red-plaid wool scarf that accompanied it, then made himself right at home by hanging them both up in the hall closet.

"You don't know how much I hate traveling," he said when that was done and he'd turned to face her once more. "Especially to California. Nothing ever changes there—the weather, the seasons, even the women all look alike," he complained. "All tall and tan and blond, like so many Barbie dolls lined up in a row."

"You could do worse, you know," Lucy pointed out lightly. Simon's good humor was infectious, and a happy smile lit her face as she led the way into the living room.

"It's perfect!" he exclaimed, pausing in the arched doorway and looking around the small room, and Lucy realized that this was the first time he had seen it. "It looks just like you."

She watched with some amusement as he explored the room thoroughly, dwarfing it with his size as he examined the handmade hooked rug, the comfortable, overstuffed furniture and the overflowing bookshelves that lined the walls.

"Are you implying that I look overstuffed?" said Lucy, raising one eyebrow humorously as she reached down to plump up the fat pillows lining the back of the couch.

"Not at all," Simon denied quickly. He leaned closer to peer at a collection of framed family photographs on one of the shelves. "I'm implying that you look warm and comfortable and welcoming, just like this room."

"Thank you—I think," Lucy said slowly. Would she never understand this man at all? Here she had tried so hard to turn herself into a sparkling sophisticate and he was telling her that all the time it was the lived-in look that turned him on.

"Can I get you something to drink?" she offered when he straightened and turned back around to face her, his perusal finished.

"In a moment," Simon said deeply, "but first . . ."

Crossing the room in three quick strides, he gathered Lucy into his arms, his dark, fathomless eyes seeking out and holding hers as his head descended slowly, so slowly that it seemed like an eternity before their lips finally touched. With calm, sure possession, his mouth closed over hers, his tongue reaching out to part her lips, then slipping inside to taste and explore the honeyed depths in an embrace so intimate, so earthshattering that Lucy could only cling mindlessly to the soft lapels of his jacket, pressing her body into the hard length of his and moaning her compliance.

"Now that," Simon murmured, his tone rife with male satisfaction, "is what I should have done last week. At least it would have shut you up."

"Me?" Lucy demanded, taking a step back and hastily trying to regain her equilibrium. Drawing herself up to her full height, she propped her hands on her hips in a position of outrage. "As I recall, Mr. Farlow, when it came to saying offensive things, you got in your share as well!"

"Slim," Simon muttered, shaking his head, "don't go all testy on me now. I was only kidding."

"Were you?" Lucy frowned uncertainly.

"Of course." Simon grinned. "Believe me, after going ten rounds with you last week, I'm in no shape for a rematch."

In spite of herself, Lucy laughed. "In that case," she said, gesturing toward the couch, "why don't you sit down and conserve your strength while I check on dinner and fix you a drink."

Taking his order, Lucy disappeared into the kitchen where everything still sat in readiness, just as she had left it only minutes before.

Calm down, she berated herself, feeling rather foolish that the preparation of one simple meal, even one being readied for a master chef himself, could have this effect on her nerves. It was foolproof—Margo had said so. What could possibly go wrong?

Running her eye over the detailed list as she splashed Scotch into two tumblers full of ice, Lucy saw that she had fifteen minutes to go before it was time to put the steaks in the oven and start the butter melting in the frying pan for the mushrooms. No problem at all, everything was under control.

With confidence adding a buoyant lift to her step, Lucy shouldered open the swinging kitchen door, delivered Simon's drink into his hands, then sat down beside him on the couch, prepared to enjoy her time to the fullest. Helping himself to the cheese and crackers, Simon told her of his latest trip to the Coast, his eyes alight with boyish enthusiasm as he described the people he had seen, the location he had scouted and the blueprints that were already beginning to take shape in his mind.

Then Duncan wandered into the room, installing himself on the floor in front of the couch, and the talk turned to dogs and Tess's upcoming litter of puppies, due in just over a month. A brief lull in the conversation several minutes later provided Lucy with the break she needed to slip away and complete her preparations—popping the steaks under the broiler in the top oven and placing the mushrooms into the pan on the stove. Whistling jauntily under her breath, she freshened their drinks, then returned to the living room once more; their conversation this time centering on her management of Sweet Tooth and the plans she was making for expansion.

It was the jarring and thoroughly unexpected sound of a small explosion from the direction of the kitchen that brought all conversation to an abrupt halt as Lucy and Simon automatically turned to look at one another in stunned surprise.

"What the hell was that?" Simon muttered, starting to rise.

"Nothing—I'm sure it was nothing!" Lucy said quickly, reaching out to push him back down on the couch as she scrambled to her feet. "Stay here. Finish your drink," she said, her eyes pleading with him silently to do as she asked. "I'll just go check on that and be right back."

Hurrying into the kitchen, Lucy quickly located the source of the problem. Pulling open the door to the lower oven, she was confronted by the sight of gooey white baked potatoes splattered everywhere—on the sides of the oven and the roof, on the rack and on the cooking elements as well. Hastily she reached up and turned off the heat. "What in the world . . . ?" she muttered, not having the slightest idea what had gone wrong. Gone were the two nice foil-wrapped potatoes she had placed in the oven earlier, replaced in one fell swoop by a sticky, dripping mess.

Her immediate thought was to clean up the evidence of the disaster before it could be discovered. Later, when that was done, she would figure out what to serve in place of the potatoes. Striding across the room, she poked her head out the kitchen door, smiling broadly in the hope of forestalling any questions Simon might have.

"Nothing wrong," she assured him brightly. "If you can manage to amuse yourself for a minute or two, I'll be right back out."

That done, she let the door swing shut behind her, then raced back across the room and yanked open the utility drawer, snatching up a knife to scrape away the mess. Kneeling on the floor, she poked her head into the fast-cooling oven and went to work. Five minutes passed, then ten. Whoever would have thought such nice fluffy potatoes could become so sticky? she thought grimly, bending to the task with all the dedication of the truly desperate. Another five minutes flew by without her even being aware of them, then finally the job was done. Rising to her feet, she gathered up the remains and dropped them into the garbage can, then wiped her palms back and forth over each other in satisfaction.

"Are you still alive in here?" Simon asked, poking his head around the swinging door before pushing it aside and admitting himself fully into the kitchen.

"Of course," Lucy said. "Everything's under control. I told you I'd be right back out, didn't I?"

"So you did." Simon nodded. "But that was almost twenty minutes ago. I thought perhaps you could use some help."

Moving closer, he peered interestedly into the oven that was still open behind her. "Little accident?" he inquired, using the tip of one finger to flick a tiny piece of potato she had overlooked on the door.

"Trivial," Lucy assured him airily, inwardly cursing her ineptitude. "Nothing to be concerned about at all."

"Aha . . ." said Simon, nodding to himself thoughtfully, "the old exploding potato trick." Looking closely, Lucy could see that he was trying hard not to smile. "I guess you forgot to prick the skins with a fork?"

Slowly, Lucy nodded. "Why would I want to do a thing like that?" she asked, her bewilderment evident in her eyes.

Unable to help himself any longer, Simon grinned broadly as he gestured toward the open oven. "I would have thought the answer was obvious."

"To you, maybe," Lucy mumbled, turning away from the laughter she saw in his eyes.

Gently Simon reached out and grasped her shoulders, bringing her back around. The look he gave her was disturbingly warm, and he explained, "You prick the holes so that the steam can escape as the potato cooks, otherwise . . ." His eloquent shrug conveyed the rest of the answer.

"Oh." Lucy frowned, assimilating this vital bit of information crossly now that it was much, much too late. "Some foolproof dinner," she muttered under her breath, talking to herself as she reached around to shut the oven. "Margo never said anything about pricking any potatoes!"

"Who's Margo?" Simon asked curiously.

"My ex–best friend," Lucy retorted, her spirit returning in a rush. After all, this was not the end of the world. Who needed potatoes anyway? The meal would do just fine without them! Why, she'd just . . .

"Lucy?" Simon said hesitantly, breaking into her thoughts.

"Yes?" Her eyes wide, she glanced up at him, his tone alerting her that something else was wrong.

"If you don't mind my asking," Simon said gently, "what's that smell?"

It was a moment before she realized what he was talking about. Then as she lifted her head and sniffed the air experimentally, Lucy's eyes widened in horror. "The steaks!" she gasped, grabbing for the nearest potholder. "I forgot all about them!"

Throwing open the door to the upper oven, she released a cloud of black smoke into the room.

"My God, woman!" Simon roared. "Don't tell me you were using the broiler with the oven door closed!" Snatching the potholder from her hand, he reached in and pulled out the broiler pan, then quickly turned off the heat.

"You don't have to shout!" Lucy cried defensively. "How was I supposed to know? Margo didn't say anything about—"

"It seems this Margo, whoever she is, has a lot to

answer for," Simon commented, his lips twitching irrepressibly as he surveyed the charred remains of their meal.

"I forgot to turn them over," Lucy mused, leaning around Simon's body to peer down over his shoulder at the steaks.

"No problem," Simon said drily, spearing one with a fork and holding it up to display the evidence. "They've cooked all the way through."

It was then that Lucy began to giggle. Her reaction was totally inappropriate to the situation, she knew, and later she would suspect that it was partly nerves that caused such an inane reaction, but she was engulfed with laughter; and what was more, once she started, she couldn't stop. It was only a moment before the deep, rich sound of Simon's laughter joined her own, and the kitchen rang with the sound of their shared merriment.

"So far, you're batting a thousand," Simon observed, walking over to the range and lifting the top off the long-forgotten mushrooms. "And I'm afraid these poor things, whatever they are, won't spoil your perfect record." Leaning down, he eyed the blackened lumps closely. "Just out of curiosity," he said, "what were they before you got hold of them?"

"Mushrooms," Lucy gasped out, still giggling, and totally unable to view this new disaster with the solemnity it deserved.

"I see." Simon nodded. Once more, he very carefully reached around and turned off the heat. "There now," he said, looking around the room like a demolitions expert, alert to any hidden dangers. "I think we've managed to defuse all your ammunition for the time being."

"So you have," Lucy agreed with a wry smile as she followed the line of his gaze around the chaotic room. "So I guess now only one question remains."

Simon arched one eyebrow upward.

"How do you feel about anchovies?"

"Never could stand the things," he admitted.

"Good," said Lucy, picking up the receiver and dialing the number of the nearest pizza parlor. "I can see you and I are going to get along just fine."

Twenty minutes later when the pizza arrived, Lucy proposed a toast. "Here's to the one thing I didn't manage to ruin," she announced with a flourish, brandishing the carafe of red wine from which she'd poured them each a glass.

"Cabernet Sauvignon and pepperoni pizza." Simon sighed, surveying the spread before him with obvious satisfaction. "Ahh, the good life!"

Despite its disastrous beginnings, the dinner that followed was a riotous affair. Lucy and Simon divided the spoils, passed out the napkins and ate with their fingers, the informality promoting a spell of easy intimacy under which they talked and laughed, sharing experiences and swapping stories. It wasn't until much later, when the food had been eaten and the dishes disposed of and they were once again seated side by side on the plump, cushioned couch, that Lucy became aware of the smell of burnt food still lingering in the air and was once more assailed by doubts.

"I really feel awful about all this," she said softly. "This wasn't how things were supposed to go at all."

"Really?" Simon feigned surprise. "And here I thought dinner was wonderful." His arm moved along the top of the cushion behind them, circling Lucy's shoulders and drawing her head down to nestle against his chest, his fingers burying themselves in her hair. "Why don't you tell me what you hoped the evening would be like?"

It was a moment before Lucy replied. The gentle, caressing touch of his fingers at her nape and the warm, vibrant feel of his chest beneath her cheek lulled her senses in a way that made rational thought seem like a superfluous commodity. Tenderly, she laid the palm of her hand over his heart, slipping her fingers beneath the lapel of his sports coat so that only the fine cotton weave of his shirt separated their flesh, no barrier at all to the heat they transmitted to each other.

"I'll tell you how this evening was supposed to go," she said, gently mocking herself with her own words. "To begin with, the meal was to have been a study in effortless perfection—the filet mignon medium rare, the potatoes fluffy, the mushrooms moist and succulent. You were supposed to have been bowled over by my culinary talents, not to mention my efficiency, as you savored every last morsel to the fullest."

Lucy felt Simon's chuckle even before she heard it, the deep rumbling in his chest alerting her to what was to come. Drawing her head away though her hand still remained in place, she looked up at him, her cobalt eyes opened wide with reproach.

"Slim," Simon said softly, shaking his head, "I came here to spend the evening with *you*, not Suzy Homemaker. Dinner was perfect just the way it was." Seeing that she was still unconvinced, he added, "That other meal you planned would have been enjoyable certainly, but don't you see, we had all that and more . . ."

Lucy blinked rapidly several times. "Did we?"

All at once, Simon looked impossibly stern. "What you need," he said firmly, "is a good, strong dose of self-confidence. So you can't cook, who cares? Nobody's perfect."

When she didn't reply, Simon cupped her chin in the palm of his hand, tilting her head back so that he could look deeply into her eyes. "You have to let go of the past," he murmured. "It's stopping you from being all that you can be today. When are you going to accept the fact that you are a beautiful, accomplished woman? What will it take to make you believe?"

Safe in the protective shelter of his arms, Lucy moaned softly. "I want to believe that, Simon, but that's not the way that I feel. Sometimes, when I look into a mirror, all I see is the past."

"If only you could see yourself as I see you," he whispered, pulling her forward into his arms. "Trust me, Slim, you're beautiful."

"I do trust you, Simon," Lucy murmured, giving herself up to the seductive pleasure of his embrace. "Oh, Simon, make me believe . . ."

With a groan that started deep in his throat, Simon's mouth came down to capture hers, his lips moving with a gentle, searching insistence that melted away the last of Lucy's doubts and fanned the glowing embers of desire that were already smoldering within. She quivered slightly as he moved above her, shifting his weight so that she lay beneath him, pressed into the soft, yielding cushions of the couch, and reveling in the entrapment. Her lips parted beneath his as she welcomed his tongue with her own, and their mouths came together as one, exploring each other's secret depths with joyful abandon.

"Oh God, Slim," Simon whispered, his lips moving across her face and throat in a succession of light, feathery kisses. "I want to go slowly with you, but you make it hard, very hard."

"Yes," Lucy murmured wickedly, arching her body upward so that her hips ground against his. "I know."

"Witch," Simon growled, surprise in his voice, and pleasure. Slowly his fingers slipped down along the side of her body until his hand found her breast. Throbbing with sensation, it swelled into his palm, and Lucy moaned softly as his thumb swirled over the taut material covering the sensitive peak.

Wiggling deliciously beneath him, she tugged at the

buttons of his shirt, pulling the material free of the waistband and pushing it aside so that she could feel the heat of his skin against her own. Her fingers trembled with delight as they curled into the rough mat of hair covering his chest, playing over the warm, strong muscles, then moving downward to trace the smooth spiral of hair that trailed down his stomach and disappeared beneath his belt.

Simon shuddered violently, his breathing deep and ragged. When his lips found hers once more, there was no gentleness in his kiss, only compelling, masterful intent; but Lucy was beyond the need for gentle persuasion now, swept along on a tide of sensation that awakened an aching deep inside, an elemental yearning that threatened to rise up and consume her with its overwhelming fire.

Eagerly Lucy rose to meet him, linking her fingers behind his neck and holding his lips to hers with a feverish, impatient longing that could not be denied. Slowly his fingers moved to the delicate buttons of her blouse, unfastening each with a calm, measured deliberation that belied his impatience. Sensing his hesitation, Lucy realized suddenly that he was unsure. She had stopped him at this point once before, and now he was giving her time to think, to decide for herself whether or not she was ready to move on.

At the thought of his consideration, a wave of tenderness washed over her. She could no more call a halt to Simon's lovemaking than she could order the moon from the sky; for she knew now with an irrefutable certainty that this was what she wanted. They would share each other's bodies as they had shared each other's thoughts, for he was the one man who knew her almost as well as she knew herself. He had seen her at her best, and he had seen her at her worst, yet still, he accepted her for what she was.

"Please," she whispered, responding to his unspoken plea, "touch me, Simon." His answering growl lit a spark within her, and Lucy's body seemed to melt beneath the potent magic of his touch, turning to liquid fire.

The silk rustled softly as Simon pushed the edges of her shirt aside. "Mmm . . . much better," he murmured at the sight of her bra, the champagne satin one he had chosen himself, and Lucy smiled softly, warmed by his approval. "And ever so easy to get rid of," he added, doing just that. His fingers unhooked the front clasp, then gently smoothed the lace aside.

For a moment, he held himself away, raised up on one elbow and gazed down at her warmly, reveling in the sight of her half-naked body. Another time such long, loving scrutiny would have been her undoing, but Lucy felt no embarrassment now, only a dawning sense of wonder that her body could ignite the smoldering depths of passion she saw in his eyes.

"You're beautiful," Simon said softly. His hand slipped upward to cup the velvet fullness of her breast, stroking it with a tantalizing caress that left Lucy limp with desire, oblivious to everything save the pulsating needs he awakened within her. Moaning softly, she gave herself up fully to the pleasure of the moment, delighting in the discovery of awesome, overwhelming sensations she had only imagined before.

"So are you," she murmured unevenly, her fingers tracing a sensual message over the hard planes of his back.

"I want you," said Simon, bending his head low and trailing his lips provocatively down her throat. "I must have you."

He slid down beside her on the couch, and his mouth moved lower still, the touch of his lips explosive on the soft skin of her breast. His tongue circled her rosy nipple, teasing it into hardness. Lucy shivered helplessly beneath him, feeling at that moment as though he possessed her totally. Body and soul, she was his, and his alone.

"I want you too, Simon," she whispered.

In a single fluid motion, Simon rose to his feet, then bent down and lifted her into his arms, cradling her gently as he strode across the room and down the narrow hallway on the other side. "Nothing like a man who knows his way around," Lucy mumbled dreamily under her breath, pressing herself close against the warm, comforting wall of his body and delighting in the feel of his hair-roughened chest against her cheek. She breathed in deeply, inhaling the heady, musky scent that was uniquely his own.

Pausing at the door to the first bedroom, Simon looked down at her quizzically, and she nodded. Firmly he shouldered aside the door, then carried her into the darkened room, which was lit only by the long stream of light from the hallway. Crossing the room, Simon set her down beside the bed. There, with a gentleness bordering on reverence, he slipped off the pieces of her clothing one by one, his eyes smoldering with a passion so fierce that Lucy could feel the combustible heat between them.

"Lovely, utterly lovely," Simon breathed, running his hands down the curves of her body as he lowered her slowly onto the fragrant, pale yellow sheets.

"Really?" Lucy's whispered plea was as soft as a sigh.

Gazing down at her, Simon raised one eyebrow fractionally. "Are you fishing for a compliment?" he growled, his voice husky with desire.

"Yes."

"Slim," Simon murmured, "you're beautiful. Trust me, you're all the woman a man could ever want." He straightened then and stripped off his own clothes quickly, impatiently, his eyes never leaving her for a moment.

"Please . . ." Lucy sighed, caught up in a feverish, impatient longing as he towered over her momentarily, looking like a tall, regal Adonis. Her senses reeled at the sight of his powerful, sun-bronzed body, and she was drunk with reaction, filled with a potent desire that swept fire through her veins.

"I will please you," Simon promised softly. The mattress dipped slightly, then he was beside her, taking her into his arms. "We will please each other."

His hands stroked her body with sensual expertise, coaxing her to an increasingly higher plane of passion and pleasure as they brushed over her lightly from hip to thigh. Arching upward beneath him, Lucy molded her body to his, breast to chest, thigh to thigh, skin against skin, as she drew in her breath in a deep, quivering sigh. Her senses racing wildly, she heard the pounding beat of her own heart echo in her ears and felt more fully alive at that moment than she ever had before. Her body pulsed with a demanding need of its own, aching for the final surrender.

"God, Slim," Simon said feverishly, "you don't know what you do to me."

"Don't I?" Lucy murmured, her breath ragged and uneven. "Tell me then."

Simon glowered down at her briefly, then swooped down to nibble the lobe of her ear. "You drive me crazy," he murmured, caressing her throat with a flick of his tongue. "You make me want you like I've never wanted anyone before."

All at once, Lucy felt a driving need to reciprocate, to please Simon as he was pleasing her. "Show me," she whispered, her fingertips dancing lightly over the solid expanse of his heated flesh. "Show me what you want, Simon."

She traced an intimate pattern downward, first her hands, then her lips exploring his chest, finding the small male nipples nestled amid the hairs and teasing them to awareness. Then with a boldness she had not known she possessed, she dipped lower still, caressing the flat, hard muscles of his stomach and then his hips, glorying in the burgeoning evidence of his desire.

"I want *you*," Simon groaned, his eyes black with passion. "Now."

Pressing his hands to her shoulders, Simon rolled over on top of her, the full weight of his body crushing her down into the soft mattress; but the heavy restraint only excited Lucy more, and she moved beneath him instinctively, feeling his need and guiding him to her. With a deep, anguished gasp she welcomed him; the small, momentary shock of pain was quickly swept away as though it had never been. Simon clasped her close, their bodies one and moving in unison.

Gently at first Simon rocked her, and then with growing need, as the full force of his power engulfed them both. Following his lead, Lucy was overwhelmed by the blinding force of sensations that carried her far beyond the realm of past experience. Her soul seemed to soar, weightless and free, and then suddenly the explosion came, and the world dissolved around her into a thousand different colored lights cascading down upon them. She cried out Simon's name and heard his answering response, and they clung to each other fiercely as though they would never let go.

Afterward, they lay side by side on the warm, rumpled bed, wrapped in the security of each other's arms as their bodies wound down slowly from the tumultuous physical release. Eyes closed, Lucy nestled beneath Simon's arm, resting her cheek on his broad chest, her thoughts drifting aimlessly, her body aglow with a feeling of utter contentment.

Absently she slipped her hand up over his heart once more, lulled by the throb of its strong, steady beat. Why hadn't anyone told her she would feel this incredible tenderness toward him afterward? she wondered dreamily, this sense of communion, this oneness—a bond that went far beyond the physical union they had just shared. Why hadn't she known. . . .

"It was your first time, wasn't it?" Simon said gently, raising himself up on his side and resting on one elbow so that he could look down upon her where she lay, still cradled by his other arm.

Hesitantly, unsure of his reaction, Lucy nodded.

"Why didn't you tell me?"

Silently her eyes searched his face, seeking a clue to his feelings, but finding none. "Would it have made a difference to you?" she asked softly.

For a moment, Simon considered his reply, then slowly, he shook his head. "I don't know." He paused, then added, "But I would have gone more slowly, given you more time to be sure of what you wanted."

"I was sure, Simon." Lucy breathed in deeply. Reaching up, she ran the tip of one finger lightly, caressingly down the side of his body from shoulder to thigh. "I was very sure."

An answering shudder rippled through his body as Simon bent down and kissed her, his lips moving over hers tenderly, almost soothingly, playing back and forth over the contours of her mouth, then lingering on one corner. He whispered softly, "I think I'm falling in love with you, Slim."

It was a moment before Simon's words registered in her brain, and then another several moments still before she was able to discern their meaning. Simon falling in love? It wasn't possible! Then, abruptly, she realized what he was doing.

In this, as in everything else, he was expert, she mused silently. Even in the aftermath of love, he was still the perfect ladies' man, still the perfect gentleman, doing everything he could to ensure that this was a pleasurable experience for her; even down to uttering that final, time-honored declaration. His motives were quite simple, really, Lucy decided. She had confessed her innocence, and he had felt honor-bound to reassure her with talk of love.

All at once, she felt overwhelmed by tenderness. How thoughtful Simon was to try to comfort her that way, as if the simple words themselves could make everything all right. No matter that the line he'd used was old as time, Lucy was touched by his consideration, and captivated. Caught up in the spell of quiet euphoria that surrounded them, she felt a compelling need to reassure him as well.

Gazing up at him, she smiled indulgently. "You don't have to say that," she said, wanting to let him know that he needn't feel guilty—that he hadn't taken anything from her, for everything they'd shared she had freely offered to him.

Looking somewhat taken aback by her answer, Simon frowned. "I know I don't have to," he said slowly. "I want to."

But to Lucy, the comment, which she knew was meant to be comforting, only hurt all the more. He's humoring me, she thought. He doesn't think I'm enough of an adult to handle this.

"Shh," she murmured. Placing her fingertips gently over his lips to silence him, then replacing them with her mouth, she drew him back once more into the realm of elemental communication where no words were needed.

Later, much later, after they had again found the heights to which their passion could take them, Lucy lay back amid the rumpled bedcovers, her body enveloped in a state of dreamy languor that demanded sleep as its release. Snuggling drowsily down into the pillow, she was stunned when Simon slipped out of the other side of the bed and began looking about for his discarded clothing.

"What are you doing?" she mumbled, pushing herself up into a sitting position, then realized that the answer was perfectly obvious and amended her question. "Where are you going?"

"Home." Simon leaned down and kissed her gently, but the smile he bestowed upon her looked forced.

"Home?" Lucy echoed in wounded disbelief. He was leaving *now*? Watching in silence while Simon pulled on his clothes, she clutched the blankets to her chin, overcome by confusion as she pondered his sudden withdrawal. How could he possibly be so cool? she wondered. Had he no feelings at all?

"Will I see you tomorrow?" she asked, hating the sound of desperation in her words. "It's Sunday, and I don't have to work. Maybe we could spend the day together?"

For a single, heart-stopping second, she thought he was going to refuse. Then Simon looked down at her, wrapped amid the bedcovers, utterly vulnerable to his wishes, and he nodded.

"Tomorrow," he promised softly, then disappeared through the door.

8

Lucy rose early the next morning, and she had already
been up for several hours by the time she heard the
steady hum of the Porsche's motor, signaling Simon's
arrival. Jumping up from her seat at the kitchen table, she
tossed aside the Sunday *New York Times Magazine*
crossword puzzle, then quickly gathered the paper's
myriad other sections into some semblance of order.
Ducking into the powder room on her way to answer the
door, she scanned the image in the mirror anxiously and
was satisfied by what she saw.

Unsure of how the day was to be spent, she had taken
a leaf from Simon's book and dressed casually in a pair of
black denim designer jeans and a white Fair Isle sweater
with a beautifully patterned yoke in muted pastel shades
of pink and blue. Though she wore hardly any makeup,
her cheeks glowed with healthy color, lit from within by
the same thrill of anticipation that had her bright blue
eyes sparkling happily.

Throwing open the front door, she found Simon already on the step, his hand poised in midair as though he were just about to knock. Unexpectedly her breath lodged in her throat, and for a moment Lucy could only stand and stare, bowled over anew by the compelling attraction she felt for this man. Her gaze skimmed over him lightly, and she noted that he had dressed much the same way she had, wearing well-worn jeans and a faded, red-striped rugby shirt.

Then his eyes found hers, and their gazes locked. Briefly Lucy was sure she read appreciation, even approval, in his face. Then it was gone, replaced by a shuttered look she could not read at all, and Simon was pulling her forward into his arms for a quick, unsatisfying kiss. His lips were chaste, almost fraternal, as they moved over hers in a welcoming caress.

"Good, you're all ready," he said, straightening and moving back a step to put some space between them. "Then we can leave right away."

"Yes, we can if you like." Lucy frowned uncertainly. "Where are we going?"

Reaching around behind her, Simon pulled the front door shut, dispelling any thoughts she might have had about inviting him in for a cup of coffee or even going back to retrieve her purse.

"I thought we might take a drive up through northern Connecticut into Massachusetts," Simon explained as he ushered her into the car. "Now that the leaves have turned, the foliage up in the Berkshires is breathtaking. People come from all over this time of year to drive through and appreciate nature's glorious colors. It seems silly for us to miss it when we're so close by."

"Yes, it does," Lucy agreed absently, settling into the leather seat. "That sounds like a wonderful idea."

What in the world is the matter with him? she wondered, her mind working over the problem furiously.

Why is he acting this way? So formal, even businesslike, almost as though they were strangers, when, especially after last night, they were anything but.

He had certainly hurried her out of the house fast enough, Lucy mused, frowning. It was almost as if he felt that the sooner he got things started, the sooner they would be over. Was he sorry they were going to be spending the day together? She slanted a glance out of the corner of her eye at his strong, clean profile. He almost looked that way. But why? What was going on?

"Is something wrong?" she asked, turning in the bucket seat to face him.

"No," Simon said evenly, shaking his head. "Why do you ask?"

"I don't know." Lucy shrugged, unwilling to put her feelings into words but unnerved by them all the same. "I guess you just seem preoccupied."

"Do I?" Simon smiled briefly, and it took Lucy's breath away. "I don't mean to be. I'm just concentrating on my driving, that's all."

No, that isn't all! Lucy's mind screamed in furious denial, but she did not voice her thoughts. Whatever it was that was bothering Simon, he was just going to have to work it out for himself, because it was clear that he didn't want her help!

Heading north on Route 7, the silver Porsche quickly ate away the miles. After the first hour and a half of driving, they reached the more rural areas of northern Connecticut. The road twisted and narrowed as they drove along the rushing Housatonic River, then widened once more when they came to open farmland, acre after acre of post-and-rail-bound pastures dotted with grazing horses and cows. They paused atop several hills offering panoramic views of the surrounding countryside, but to none of these did Lucy give the attention and appreciation they deserved. For Simon's sake, she oohed and aahed at appropriate moments, but her eyes saw little of the sights she exclaimed over. Her thoughts were still turned inward and whirling in bitter confusion.

It was almost as if he were angry with her, Lucy decided, as the miles slipped by and still Simon continued to maintain his cool façade. But that didn't make any sense. What could he possibly have to be angry about, and why now of all times? Last night she had given him what he wanted, what all men like him wanted. This morning he should have been feeling smug, or sated, or even triumphant—she could have handled any of those attitudes. In fact, she could have handled almost anything except what he was actually doing—sitting across from her as cool and unapproachable as an iceberg. It was as if their truly wonderful experience the night before had meant nothing to him, as if the lovemaking they had shared was the sort of commonplace, everyday thing that happened to him all the time.

Abruptly Lucy gulped as a large lump rose in her throat, making breathing suddenly difficult. That was it exactly—the issue she'd been skirting around, but hadn't wanted to face. With his reputation, it probably did happen to him all the time. She'd been a novelty for him, but certainly nothing out of the ordinary. Unaccountably that thought hurt, the pain searing down deep into her heart.

Fool! Lucy berated herself. You were the one who wanted a man with experience, and that's exactly what you got. So you can hardly turn around and blame him now for running true to type—for being the sort of man who could make love to a woman without it meaning anything to him. Staring blindly out of the window beside her, Lucy sighed. Today she felt closer to Simon than ever before, yet he only seemed to be moving further and further away. If this was what sophistication meant, she mused grimly, denying your true feelings, acting outwardly cool when inside you were glowing with warmth, then she didn't want any part of it!

In midafternoon, they stopped for lunch at a sprawling, outdoor country market that sold everything from fruits and vegetables to homemade pastries to Indian corn. Munching on hot dogs and sipping thick, sweet apple cider from paper cups, they wandered up and down the aisles, poring over the various displays.

For the first time all day, Simon seemed to relax. Grinning at her enthusiasm, he held out a small wicker basket for Lucy to fill with shiny Red Delicious apples. A jug of cider and a wreath made of dried Indian corn also found their way into his arms, and she giggled delightedly at the sight he made—the classic picture of a long-suffering male overburdened by an unexpected shopping spree.

"So you think this is funny, do you?" Simon growled with mock ferocity as he looked down at his heavily laden arms. "There only seems to be one thing missing here, and I'll tell you what it is, a little equality of the sexes!" With that, he delivered the basket of apples into her waiting arms. Then, cradling their other purchases easily on one side, Simon reached out to take her hand, the firm grasp of his fingers warm and reassuring as they entwined with hers. Lucy smiled happily.

Finally, she thought with an inward sigh of relief. Now everything will be all right.

Their good humor carried them back to the car, where their supplies were neatly stowed away in the space behind the seats. Simon came around and unlocked her door, but before Lucy could climb in her attention was caught by three young children, obviously siblings, who were arguing loudly over the selection of a Halloween pumpkin. Watching their friendly rivalry as they debated the merits of almost every pumpkin on the lot, Lucy's expression softened.

Simon turned, then smiled as his gaze followed hers. "Kids are great, aren't they? They're so full of life and enthusiasm that even an outing to buy a pumpkin can become a great adventure."

"Of course," Lucy agreed, returning his smile. "After all, making a jack-o'-lantern is no easy task. Don't you remember from when you were little? If you didn't get exactly the right pumpkin, the candle wouldn't stand up straight, the eyes would go crooked—why, all sorts of things could go wrong."

"Actually," Simon drawled wickedly, "when I was little, I was more apt to be smashing jack-o'-lanterns than carving them out."

"Shame on you!" Lucy cried, entering into their first unstilted conversation of the day with spirit. "What a nasty child you must have been! Don't tell me you stuck pins in doorbells and tied cans to cats' tails as well?"

Simon nodded sheepishly. "The doorbells, maybe," he admitted, "but I left the cats alone. As you may have noticed, I have quite a soft spot for animals."

"I'm glad to hear that you weren't totally incorrigible," Lucy teased. "I suppose there may be hope for you yet."

"There," said Simon, nodding in the direction of the children. "They've finally found it, the perfect pumpkin."

"So they have." Lucy grinned. As she continued to watch, the children rejoined their parents and were now engaged in arguing over who was to be the one to carry their prize home.

"You look almost envious," Simon commented, his brown eyes twinkling. "Does this mean I have to buy you a pumpkin, too?"

"No thanks." Lucy shook her head, her face taking on an unconsciously wistful expression as she watched the happy family leave.

"Well then?" Simon prompted curiously.

"Actually," she admitted, "I was thinking about the children."

Simon groaned loudly. "You want me to buy you children?"

In spite of herself, Lucy giggled. "Don't be ridiculous," she bantered back. "Don't you know that the best children are still made the good, old-fashioned way?"

"What nice thoughts you have," Simon growled under his breath, his mouth close to her ear as he handed her into the car. "You see," he commented a moment later, settling into his own seat beside her, "we're in perfect agreement. I'm looking forward to making babies, and you're looking forward to having them!"

"Yes, of course I am," Lucy replied, her light, teasing tone matching Simon's own, "but not right this minute. I mean, there are a few small details that need to be ironed out first . . ."

"Oh?" Simon cocked one eyebrow humorously. "You mean like getting our clothes off, finding a bed, 'your place or mine,' that sort of thing?"

"Not exactly." Lucy laughed. "Actually I was thinking more of the fundamentals—like love and marriage, and finding that one special man to spend the rest of my life with."

Lucy was looking out through the windshield while Simon pulled back onto the road, so she didn't see the exact moment when his mood changed, but as soon as she heard his voice, she knew that it had.

"That sounds like an ongoing search," he commented, his voice flat and surprisingly cool, and Lucy glanced up quickly, startled by his tone.

He was making fun of her again, she realized suddenly, her heart plummeting. First her clothes, then her cooking, and now this! Lucy's shoulders stiffened defiantly. Maybe her ideals did seem a little old-fashioned to a man who lived the type of life that Simon did, but they were hers, and she wasn't about to apologize for them!

"It is," she declared, deliberately matching his cool, detached tone with one of her own.

Beside her, Simon's features hardened angrily, and his foot pressed down hard on the accelerator in a way that sent the responsive Porsche shooting forward, speeding them toward home.

Now what had she done? Lucy wondered, settling back in her seat with a weary sigh. Was there no understanding this man at all?

As on the ride out, silence prevailed, with Simon retreating behind a mask of icy reserve that precluded any overtures Lucy might have made. With each passing mile, she grew crosser and crosser, frustrated by her inability to read Simon's mind and his apparent lack of desire to enlighten her. Going over the scene at the market in her mind, Lucy could come to only one conclusion—everything had been fine until their conversation had turned, by chance, to the subject of marriage. That was what, for some reason, had angered him all over again.

Maybe the problem went beyond his not feeling anything for her, she decided. Perhaps he was actually regretting what had happened between them, afraid that she might somehow try to trap him into a commitment he didn't want to make. After all he was well known to be the "love 'em and leave 'em" type. Maybe that was why he hadn't wanted to bother spending the day with her—because he'd already gotten everything he wanted the night before! That would certainly explain his mood, at any rate. As far as he was concerned, they were finished, and it was only the guilt he felt over her lost virginity that had made him agree to drag things out by spending today with her!

Well, bully for him! Lucy thought irritably. How dare

he blow into her life like that, then turn around and make plans to blow right back out again? Who made him king for a day? Maybe she wasn't finished with him, had he ever stopped to consider that? He may have already loved her, but she'd be damned if he'd leave her, not just yet anyway!

There had to be some way to penetrate that thick hide of his, she mused, then smiled as her ever active mind supplied the obvious answer. Of course! So they didn't appear to be having much luck talking to each other, so what? Words weren't everything! There was another level of communication on which they'd operated just fine. All she had to do was find a way to get them back there again. Last night it had been Simon's turn to call the shots; today it would be hers. She would wait until they got home and then turn on the charm. After all, she had learned that trick from a master!

Regrettably, however, Lucy's plan contained one basic flaw. She had forgotten to take into account the presence of a large, enthusiastic and over-eager poodle who, having been cooped up in the house for the better part of the day, was only too pleased to throw a monkey wrench into the works.

Stepping up to the back door, Lucy unlocked and opened it, then immediately turned back around, a provocative smile playing about her lips as she reached out to trail her fingers down Simon's arm. She intended to ask him inside in a low, seductive tone that would clearly insinuate that she was not about to take no for an answer. The question, however, was never uttered, for no sooner had the door swung open than Duncan launched himself out, his enthusiastic leap bringing his paws between Lucy's shoulder blades and sending her flying forward into Simon's arms.

This still might work, she thought hopefully, not about to give up yet. Ad-libbing like mad, she allowed her body to press forward suggestively, then waited for Simon to take his cue. But to her chagrin, no embrace was forthcoming. Instead she was grasped rather firmly by the tops of her arms and set stiffly on her feet.

"Damn dog," Simon muttered under his breath, pushing the poodle away as well.

"Don't you yell at my dog!" Lucy snapped, venting the outrage she couldn't quite express on her own behalf by leaping to her poodle's defense. "Whatever's the matter with you, you don't have to take it out on him. He was only trying to be friendly."

"You're right," Simon agreed quickly, so quickly that Lucy should have known there would be a catch. Glowering down at her, he added, "An ill-behaved dog is his owner's responsibility!"

At that moment, Lucy understood the meaning of the phrase "to see red." Already the day had been agonizingly long and uncomfortable—and none of it had been her fault. This, coming on top of everything else, was simply the last straw!

"I suppose Tess is just perfect?" she shot back sharply.

"She's a damn sight closer to it than this animal!"

Angrily Lucy pushed past him and into the house. "I'd ask you in," she snapped, "but Duncan tends to be uncomfortable with people who don't like him. I'm sure you'll understand, he doesn't allow just anyone into his house."

"That's just fine with me," Simon growled, pivoting on his heel. Before there was time to say another word, he had marched back across the driveway and climbed into his car.

Well, *that* didn't resolve anything, Lucy thought angrily, standing in the doorway as the Porsche roared away. No talking, no communication, no nothing. Clearly what Simon needed was some time alone to cool off and come to grips with whatever was bothering him. And if that was what he wanted, Lucy thought irritably, then she'd be only too glad to give it to him. Who wanted to spend more time in the company of that ill-tempered lout anyway?

With that disastrous episode still regrettably fresh in her mind, Lucy felt disappointment but no surprise when several days slipped by and the only word she had of Simon came not from the man himself, but rather from her assistant. It was with great reluctance that Margo, whose ear was tuned to the fine inner workings of New Canaan's social life, informed her that Simon had been seen out and about every night that week, accompanied by a variety of different ladies.

"I hate like anything to be the one to tell you this," Margo had said, frowning apologetically, "but I thought maybe it was better if you heard it here first."

"Really, it's all right," Lucy reassured her, but even to her own ears the words rang false. "Simon and I don't have any sort of exclusive arrangement, you know that."

"The man's a louse!" Margo declared with feeling.

"Mmm, you may be right," Lucy agreed, wondering absently why she couldn't raise a more vehement condemnation of Simon's character. "Still and all," she mused aloud, "he does have some redeeming qualities."

"I'll bet," her assistant said meaningfully, "and it's obvious you're not the only one who thinks so. You should see what these bimbos look like!"

"Mar-go," Lucy intoned warningly, "I don't want to hear it!"

But her assistant was undeterred, and the juicy, descriptive details of Simon's beautiful companions followed as Lucy strode away down the hall to her office, stopping only when she slammed the door firmly behind her.

So Simon Farlow was once more on the prowl, was he? she thought grimly. Well, she'd just see about that!

Sitting down at her desk, she picked up the telephone receiver then replaced it, drumming her fingers irritably on the smooth wood surface. The last time she'd sat around wondering if Simon was going to call, he'd berated her for not calling him. Well, here she was again in exactly the same situation and she still didn't have the nerve to do it!

She had been spending a lot of time thinking about Simon lately, of that there could be no doubt. Unaccountably his absence seemed to have left a gaping hole in her life, one that had never been in evidence before. Actually Lucy had always thought she was the sort of person who didn't need other people much. She'd cherished her independence and her privacy, reveling in the time that she spent alone, with no one but Duncan for company. But now, somehow, all that had changed.

She missed Simon, Lucy admitted to herself truthfully. She missed the way he made her laugh and the way he made her think. But most of all, she missed the way he made her feel.

Lucy knew she'd always been a stubborn person by nature—stubborn enough to stick to her diet and lose the weight despite all odds against her success; stubborn enough to persevere and open her own store when others her age were satisfied with anonymous job security in a large corporation; and now she found she was just stubborn enough to want to give one more try to putting things right between them. After all, when she and Simon had been good together, they had been very good. Maybe, just maybe, she thought, there was a chance that they could be that way again.

The decision made, Lucy's resolve returned in a rush. She picked up the receiver once more, remembering as she did so this time that Simon had once mentioned an interest in taking up jogging in order to improve his endurance for other sports. It was perfect! she decided, just the excuse she needed. It took only a moment to leave the message on his machine, and in the end, the jogging date was confirmed without their ever speaking to each other at all, for Margo took the call when she was out and relayed the message of Simon's acceptance.

Perhaps the fiasco that followed was all her own fault, Lucy was to think later. If only she hadn't been so nervous, so on edge with Simon, feeling rattled and unsure; then becoming angry because of the debilitating effect his mere presence seemed to have on her sanity. If only she could have remained cool, calm and collected, maybe none of it would have happened. But she couldn't, and it did.

Still, no matter what the provocation, there was simply no excuse for what she did. It had seemed like such a good idea at the time. But later she would greatly regret the malicious impulse that goaded her to lead Simon at a fast, near-running clip around the full length of her five-mile route when, on his first time out, he was clearly in no shape for such a jaunt. She told herself that her actions were justified, that she was doing it in remembrance of their ill-fated tennis game. So he thought she was entirely without physical skills, did he? Well, she'd show him that there were some things that she could do, and do quite handily! But deep inside Lucy knew there was more to it, a tiny streak of selfish vindictiveness that wanted to see Simon put through the wringer, that wanted to pay him back in some measure for the way he had treated her.

Though the run started out exactly as she had planned, to Lucy's surprise she found as time went on that her anger was slowly giving way to grudging admiration. One mile slipped into the next, and even as they reached the four-mile point, Simon still continued to dog her footsteps without complaint. She'd thought by now he would have said something—asked to stop and walk a bit, or maybe reduce their speed—but no, he was simply toughing it out. The light conversation that had marked the first half of the run had long since given way to stoic silence as, especially during the past few minutes, Simon seemed to need his breath for other, more important things, like breathing.

He's not going to give up, is he? mused Lucy, thinking back once more to their afternoon of tennis. She'd been the first to admit that she didn't know how to play his game, but it was clear now that he had no intention of owning up to the fact that he couldn't handle hers. If that was the way he wanted to go, then so be it!

"Only one more mile," Lucy called back over her shoulder cheerfully.

His unintelligible answer fell somewhere between a grunt and a groan.

"Feeling tired yet?" she asked, her eyes glinting wickedly. From experience with trying to stretch her own boundaries, Lucy knew exactly how he must be feeling right now—as if his feet were made of lead and his thighs like knives of white-hot pain, his overtaxed muscles screaming for relief.

"A little," Simon muttered under his breath, and Lucy smiled inwardly, thinking of the beating his macho self-image must be taking right now. Imagine, she chortled silently, the ignominy of being run into the ground by a mere woman!

Staring fixedly ahead as she set the pace, Lucy didn't look back at Simon for several minutes. Then, glancing over her shoulder, she saw for the first time the lines of pain and fatigue etched across his face; immediately her heart went out to him, the grand plans she had harbored for retaliation seeming petty and childish. Suddenly the sweet taste of revenge had a decidedly sour flavor.

"Okay, that's it. We're done," she announced, reaching out with one hand to grasp his arm and pull him to a halt by the side of the road. "Time for a rest."

Looking down at her, Simon's gaze narrowed fractionally. "I thought you said we had another mile to go," he accused, although Lucy noticed he made no attempt to shake off her restraining arm.

"I did . . . we do," she stammered. Watching his powerful chest heave mightily while his tortured lungs struggled for breath, she winced, feeling the pain as surely as he must be feeling it himself. Thinking fast, she added, "I always like to walk the last mile or so. It gives me a chance to wind down slowly."

Silently Simon nodded, accepting her explanation, though Lucy privately suspected that he didn't have enough energy left to do anything else.

"Come on," she said, nodding to a path that cut through a small patch of woods—a shortcut she never used, although he wouldn't know that. "It's this way."

By the time they arrived back at the house, Simon was breathing normally once more, and the unhealthy flush mottling his face was receding. Lucy, however, was more ill at ease than ever. Usually she found running to be a great reliever of stress, but today it seemed as though the tension between them had been growing rather than diminishing as time went on.

There was a vague, impalpable feeling of friction in the air—a cool wall of formality that Simon had erected between them. She didn't understand it, and she didn't know how to combat it, and in the end, it was this very uncertainty that goaded her on.

"So," she said, ushering him through the back door into the kitchen, "did you enjoy your run?"

"I did," Simon said slowly, "very much. It was, shall we say, quite illuminating."

"What's that supposed to mean?" Lucy demanded

suspiciously. Did he realize she had taken pity on him and cut the route short?

"I mean," said Simon, helping himself to a chair, "I never realized that you had such a mean streak in you."

"Mean streak?" Lucy echoed, her blue eyes round with innocence, but Simon wasn't having any of it.

"I wasn't ready for a run of that length, and you knew it," he growled, "and enjoyed every single agonizing minute, too!"

So much for compassion, Lucy thought irritably. She never should have wasted her time feeling sorry for him.

"You could have stopped me any time," she pointed out.

"Perhaps I didn't want to spoil your fun."

"Or perhaps you didn't want to tarnish that macho image of yours by admitting that you couldn't keep up!" Lucy cried, feeling utterly frustrated by his continuing refusal to discuss what was on his mind. "You know I've just about had it with your strong, silent act!"

"What's that supposed to mean?" Simon's voice was ominously quiet, and if Lucy had been paying attention to such things, she would have realized she was treading on dangerous ground. As it was, however, she was far too angry to take notice.

"I'll tell you what it means," she blurted out. "Your whole problem is that you can't admit you're not perfect, that something might actually be bothering you! At least I accept my limitations."

"You not only accept your limitations," Simon fired right back, "you revel in them!"

"I do not!" Lucy shouted, outraged. What was he talking about? she wondered. Was this his way of telling her that she hadn't been good enough for him in bed? That if she had had more knowledge and experience, had known better how to please him, he wouldn't be running around with other women now? At that thought, a searing shaft of pain seemed to plunge deep into her heart.

"I suppose that's the logic you use to justify things to yourself," she said coolly, marshaling all her precarious self-control. If it killed her, she was not going to let him see how incompetent, how inadequate, he had just made her feel.

"What things?" said Simon, watching her closely. "What are you talking about?"

"Really, Simon, you don't have to play innocent with me. You're certainly well enough known in this town that if you decide to drown yourself in the attention of some big-busted, blond bimbos, people will notice and talk about it."

"Big-busted bimbos?" Simon repeated, and Lucy could swear he was biting back a smile.

"I'm only repeating what I hear," she informed him airily, her expression clearly indicating that she couldn't care less.

"Slim?" Simon said softly, and Lucy looked up, surprised. It seemed like an eternity since he had called her by that name. "Are you jealous?"

"No, of course not," she denied quickly, then recanted, knowing even as she did so that her defenses were tumbling about her ears. "Maybe just a little."

"Hmm," Simon murmured, stroking his chin thoughtfully. "What makes you think you have the right to be jealous?"

The question was so unexpected that for a brief moment Lucy almost laughed. As if jealousy was something that could be invoked or discarded at will! "What right do I need?" she asked cautiously.

"Well," said Simon, pausing as if to consider his answer very carefully, "if, for example, you and I were emotionally involved or were committed to one another in some way, then in that case, I suppose you would have every right to comment on how I spend my time."

"We certainly don't have anything like that!" Lucy denied quickly, remembering all too well that it was a chance reference to commitment that had so angered him once before. That was one trap she wasn't going to fall into again!

"Besides," she declared, anger overcoming good sense as she stooped to strike back at him the same way he had struck at her, "you must have some inflated idea of your own prowess if you think that after one night in bed together, I'm going to fall for you like a ton of bricks!"

"Well, then." Simon shrugged coolly, his emotions held tightly in check. "If you feel nothing for me, why shouldn't I continue to see other women whenever I want?"

"Because . . . because . . ." Lucy sputtered furiously.

"Yes?"

"Because I don't like it, that's why!" she all but shouted, but to Lucy's utter amazement, her angry outburst only made Simon grin.

Reaching up, he grasped her hand, then pulled her down onto his lap and into his arms. "If it bothers you so much," he whispered, his lips so close to her ear Lucy could feel the warmth of his breath on her cheek, "why don't you try to reform me?"

Abruptly Lucy jerked back as though she had been stung. Of all the things she had expected him to say, that was certainly *not* on the list. He was playing with her, she realized suddenly, toying with her like a fish on the end of a line. His actions had already indicated that she, by herself, hadn't been enough for him. He still wanted to play the field; all he really meant to do now was to ensure she was going to be one of the willing members of the team! To that end, he was offering himself up as some sort of prize for which they might compete. The implication of his words was clear—if she were good enough, she might be able to garner exclusive rights, at least for a little while. And if not . . .

In one smooth, fluid movement, Lucy twisted out of his grasp and rose to her feet. "I don't want to reform you!" she snapped, her cobalt eyes flashing in outrage. "Drunks and criminals and junkies—they're the sort of people who need to be reformed! Not little boys, like you, who don't know when to grow up!"

"Little boy?" Simon growled, rising to his feet as well. "Lady, have you ever got the wrong idea!"

Before she even knew what was happening, he had pulled her forward into his arms, her body locked against his hard, implacable length as his lips ground down upon hers with a forceful, crushing intensity unlike anything Lucy had ever known.

"No!" she cried breathlessly, yanking her head back and turning her face away. She lashed out at him with her foot, but Simon simply sidestepped the thrust, then pushed her back until she was pinned against the counter, trapped in place by the pressure of his body, and powerless to resist.

"Yes," he said firmly, threading his fingers through her hair as he cupped her head and turned it back to his. Then his lips found hers once more, but this time there was a difference. Gone was the force he had used before, its place taken by a gentle, coaxing hunger, which was infinitely more dangerous in its attraction. Sensing her weakening resolve, Simon loosened his hold. One small remaining spark of rationality rose to the fore, overruling her drugged senses and insisting that she break free of the embrace. Quickly, before there was time to question the act, Lucy complied, her anger bubbling dangerously close to the surface.

"Men!" she snapped, planting her hands firmly on her hips. "You think a few kisses can solve everything! I suppose now you're satisfied!"

"Oh no," said Simon, grinning broadly, the mocking gleam in his eye insinuating quite clearly what he was thinking. "There are several more things yet to be done before I'll actually be *satisfied*."

"Not with me, you won't!" Lucy declared, taking a defensive step backward. "Not now, and not ever!"

"You don't mean that," Simon said, and Lucy's fingers itched with the urge to slap the arrogant expression from his face.

"I most certainly do! You are one of the most irritating, ill-mannered men I have ever met! And I'll tell you something else," Lucy raged. "Tess must have spoiled you with all that unselfish devotion of hers because you haven't even the slightest idea how to have a real relationship with someone. You don't want a woman, Simon, all you really need is another dog!"

"That's it," Simon muttered, his voice ominously low. "I've had just about all I'm going to take from you."

"Does that mean you're leaving?" Lucy inquired sweetly, striding across the kitchen and yanking open the back door to aid him on his way.

"Yes!"

"Good!" She dusted off her palms, one against the other. "Then you'll save me the trouble of throwing you out!"

Without so much as another glance in her direction, Simon walked through the open door, and Lucy took great delight in slamming it behind him.

"And stay out!" she muttered under her breath, but the show of defiance was short-lived for with his departure, the electrically charged atmosphere fueling her anger seemed to dissipate as well.

Almost against her will she was drawn to the window, where one hand reached up tentatively, the fingers holding back the filmy curtain as she pressed her face to the cool glass and watched him walk away. Suddenly and quite without warning, a terrible feeling of desolation swept over her; she remained standing, rooted to the spot, long after the silver Porsche had disappeared from view.

Now what? she wondered bleakly, the curtain settling back into place as her hand fell to her side. Possessed by an almost eerie sense of calm, she walked woodenly into the living room and curled up into a small ball in the corner of the couch, feeling angry and hurt, but most of all bewildered. Where had she gone wrong? Lucy mused. How was it possible that an idea that had started out with such promise could end so miserably? Now, when it was far too late, she could see that Margo had been right all along—she had gotten in over her head, and now it was time to pay the price.

A low, snuffling sound alerted her to Duncan's presence just before his cold, wet nose was pressed hesitantly into her hand. "Come on up," she invited, patting the cushion beside her absently, but the poodle declined, turning around and trotting away, only to return moments later with his favorite ball.

"You want me to play catch with you *now?*" Lucy muttered irritably. "You must be kidding!"

Obligingly, Duncan's tail thumped up and down.

"You're not going to let me sit here and wallow in self-pity, are you?" Lucy demanded crossly, frowning as the tail continued to wag.

"Oh, all right." She sighed, accepting the ball. Maybe this was the best thing after all—to simply put Simon behind her and get on with her life. So she hadn't expected the affair to be so brief, what of it? She'd gained some experience, she told herself determinedly, and that was what she'd been after all the time, right?

"Oh well," Lucy muttered with a sigh as she followed the poodle outside. "No plan is perfect. . . ."

9

The following week, Lucy set about putting her life back in order with a vengeance. She'd been entirely too preoccupied lately, she decided. What was the matter with her anyway? Why, she had a store to run, candy to sell, a dog to support! What she didn't have was time to sit around mooning over some man!

With steely-eyed determination, she put the entire episode with Simon Farlow firmly behind her. As far as she was concerned now, the whole thing had been a terrible mistake—a passing whim that should never have been indulged. *I guess I just wasn't cut out to live my life in the fast lane,* she concluded ruefully, then plunged headlong back into her work.

Halloween passed, and the witches and pumpkins disappeared, relinquishing their place on the counter to a whole new array of seasonal selections: candy-striped gingerbread houses; plump, befeathered turkeys fashioned out of gumdrops; and model Pilgrims filled with hard candy.

"You know," Lucy mused one morning, surveying the store with a thoughtful eye, "this holiday stuff is all well and good, but I think what we really need is a new gimmick, something that will work all year round and be a big draw for the kids. Especially now that it looks like we're going to be getting the soda parlor going as well, I'd like them to start thinking of Sweet Tooth as a great place to hang out."

"What'd you have in mind?" Margo asked, knowing from long experience that the pensive expression on Lucy's face signaled wheels turning busily inside.

"Penny candy," Lucy announced, then turned to watch her friend's reaction.

"Penny candy?" Margo laughed. "In this day and age? You must be kidding!"

"Not at all," Lucy insisted. "I know that in the past we've sold only the finest quality candy and everything by the pound, but I'm sure there are plenty of things we could get that could be broken down into smaller lots—spearmint leaves, fireballs, licorice sticks, things like that. Just think, we could set up a whole display with dozens of things to choose from, just like general stores used to have years ago. I'll bet the kids will go for it like crazy!"

"It's crazy all right," Margo muttered, but she joined in the planning anyway, and the idea took shape and grew, finally blossoming into a project that succeeded beyond anything they might have hoped for. A campaign of tie-in advertising in the local paper billed Sweet Tooth as the candy store with "a return to old-fashioned values," and for days after the first ad ran, they were swamped with business. Everyone, from the kids they'd wanted to entice to their curious parents to their grandparents who remembered when—everyone, it seemed, just happened to be in the neighborhood with a nickel, a quarter or a dollar they wanted to spend.

"I'll never doubt you again," said Margo, watching in satisfaction as a businessman in a three-piece suit left clutching a brown paper bag full of fireballs in one hand and two pounds of quality butter creams in the other. "I'd never have believed this if I hadn't seen it with my own eyes."

Grinning, Lucy shrugged. "Just good common sense," she declared airily. "Everyone likes to feel that they're getting their money's worth, and when the price is only a penny, you can hardly go wrong!"

During the evenings when she went home, Lucy was less successful at holding wayward thoughts of Simon at bay, until she discovered an ice-cream-making machine at the hardware store. Soon the empty hours were spent in experimentation and invention, as she prepared for her next business undertaking by concocting new and different flavors of ice cream for Margo to sample and rate.

"It's bad enough that I work in a candy store," Margo muttered ungratefully when the sampling began, "but now you want me to eat ice cream every day as well?"

"Go on," Lucy scoffed, "you've never had a weight problem in your life, and I know it. Besides, I need an objective opinion."

To Lucy's delight, that was exactly what she got. When something didn't turn out right, her assistant pulled no punches. Mocha mint and banana fudge drew rave reviews, only to be followed by two disasters Margo cheerfully dubbed cherry dreadful and Molotov fruit cocktail as she dumped their full cardboard containers into the trash.

Three times over the next week and a half Simon phoned, leaving his messages first with Margo, and then on Lucy's answering machine at home—messages that

Lucy quite deliberately left unanswered. She had done a lot of thinking in the past ten days and had come to some conclusions that were, if not exactly palatable, at least realistic. It was one thing to contemplate having an affair with a gorgeous, sexy and eminently desirable man, she'd discovered, but still another to live through the reality of such an experience, especially when the man in question made no bones about his fidelity. Well, she had no intention of being just another pretty face in anybody's chorus line; and perhaps, said a small voice deep inside, not enough faith in herself to believe that she could hold the spotlight solo. Either way, thought Lucy, it didn't matter. There simply could be no future with a man whose ideals were poles apart from her own. It had been fun while it lasted, but now it was over.

So what if her life seemed somewhat empty right now? If she felt sad and out of sorts? Or found her thoughts wandering or her eyes filling up with tears at odd moments? She'd just have to get over it, Lucy told herself fiercely. There was no use in prolonging the inevitable. She and Simon simply weren't suited to one another, and a clean break was best for all concerned.

It was with a high degree of enthusiasm that she accepted a call from Sally Bonnel, leaping at the chance to get out of the store. She gladly turned her back on the paperwork that lay scattered across her desk and dashed off for an afternoon of location hunting. But despite her enthusiasm for the project at hand, none of the places Sally showed her seemed just right. The first was much too small; the second, inaccessible to anyone who didn't possess a car; and at the third, Lucy expressed her doubts as to whether or not the old building was structurally sound.

"I don't know," Sally admitted honestly. "We could have a builder come in and do an inspection, of course. You're not going to find something that suits you perfectly, you knew that before we started," she pointed out, her tone bordering on exasperation. "In this market, you simply can't afford to be too picky."

"I know, I'm sorry." Lucy frowned. Closing her eyes briefly, she reached up and massaged her temples with the tips of her fingers. "I don't know what's the matter with me."

Immediately, Sally's irritation was replaced by concern. "Are you feeling all right?"

"Sure," Lucy mumbled, "I'm fine. The last few weeks have just been kind of hectic, that's all. But if you don't mind, I think I've done enough looking for one day."

"Of course," Sally agreed quickly. "I'll keep an eye out, see what else I can line up, and we'll give it another try in a week or so."

She needed a diversion, Lucy decided that evening, blithely ignoring the fact that if her life was any fuller at the moment, she'd have to give up the time she used for sleeping. She needed something to do—something that was fun, and different, and interesting—something that would keep her mind off all the things she so desperately didn't want to think about.

Sitting down at the kitchen table, she was thumbing idly through the *New Canaan Advertiser* when a tiny headline caught her eye. "Dog Obedience Training Classes to Start at Ox Ridge." Unwittingly Lucy's thoughts wandered back to the afternoon when Simon had called her dog ill-behaved. Not that Duncan was, of course, she amended quickly, but maybe his training could use a bit of sprucing up. Eagerly, she skimmed through the accompanying article and realized that it was perfect, just what she was looking for. Glancing down, she checked her watch, discovering that if she and Duncan hurried, they could make it over to Darien just in time for registration.

As she'd never been to a dog-training class before,

Lucy had no idea what to expect when she entered the auditorium where the sessions were to be held. She was quite unprepared for the chaotic sight that greeted her. At least fifty dogs of all shapes and sizes were jammed into the large room, their owners ranging from a tiny girl with long blond braids holding a cocker spaniel, to a man who must have been in his eighties, accompanied by a very dignified dachshund. Instead of trotting along sedately in his usual place by her side, Duncan strained forward on his leash, eager to throw himself into the fray.

Frowning, Lucy tightened her hold on the leather strap protectively. Although most of the dogs seemed to be under control, there were a few that snapped and snarled, pulling their owners this way and that about the room as they barked at each new arrival, and she quickly decided she had no desire for her docile pet to make their acquaintance. Carefully keeping to the fringes of this melee, she made her way around to the registration desk where she filled out a card with her name and address, Duncan's name and breed, and her prior experience, which was none.

"Tonight we won't be trying to do much more than introduce ourselves and get organized," she was informed by the harried woman sitting behind the desk when she turned in her card. "I'm afraid we didn't count on drawing such a crowd, or we'd have tried to find a bigger room. If you want to take a seat—" she gestured vaguely toward a row of wooden chairs flanking the room—"the class will be getting under way in about five minutes."

Lucy nodded, then stepped away from the crowded desk, carefully keeping Duncan at her side. For a brief moment she hesitated, debating where to go—the chairs were, for the most part, already taken, yet the center of the floor was jam-packed as well. Casting a quick glance around the room for some possible breathing space, she was quite startled to lock eyes with a man apparently engaged in the same activity.

Automatically her gaze skimmed over him, noting the tall, well-built physique, the stylishly cut dark brown hair and the smoky gray eyes that gleamed at her with an interest he took no pains to hide. Abruptly Lucy's breath caught in her throat. Good God! she thought, with a hasty gulp. It was as if her image of Mr. Right, the man of her dreams, had come to life right before her eyes!

Oblivious now to the dogs and handlers eddying about her in happy confusion, Lucy could only continue to stand and stare in amazement at this total stranger who was the living, breathing embodiment of a decade and a half of fantasies. Then she frowned slightly, biting down on her lip in consternation. Where was the enchantment she'd expected to feel? The instant and total attraction that would swamp her senses and threaten her equilibrium? She should have been utterly undone by his sudden appearance, yet somehow that wasn't happening at all. Instead, the single strongest emotion she felt was not passion, but rather curiosity. What was going wrong?

It was then that he started toward her, threading his way effortlessly through the melee, though his eyes never left her for a moment. Watching him draw near, Lucy hastily worked up a welcoming smile and some enthusiasm to match. So what if her initial response hadn't been all she'd expected? The man was certainly very attractive, of that there could be no doubt. And maybe, for starters, it was enough. Besides, after a lifetime waiting for Mr. Right to appear, she'd be damned if she was going to back out now!

"Well, hello there," the dark-haired man said softly, appreciatively, when he had reached her side. "When I decided to bring Brutus in for training, I never dreamed there'd be fringe benefits like this. Perhaps dogs really are man's best friend."

"Woman's, too," Lucy returned with a laugh, mentally giving thanks that she hadn't had time to change her clothes before running off to class, and she was still wearing a very presentable silk shirtwaist dress. "I'm Lucy Whitcomb," she said, extending her hand.

"Brent Connors," he announced, his hand firm on hers, "and Brutus." He nodded downward, and Lucy followed the line of his gaze, her eyes widening incredulously.

It was, she decided, a measure of the confusion that Brent's appearance had provoked within her that she had not noticed the animal before, for the dog that accompanied him was one of the largest she had ever seen—a massive, harlequin Great Dane, whose broad shoulders stood on a level with her waist.

The shock she felt must have shown on her face, for Brent grinned at her stunned expression. "I know, I know, I've heard it all before—'that's not a dog, it's a pony.' But don't worry," he said, his voice pitched disarmingly low as if his words were meant for her ears alone, "once you get to know him, he's a real softie."

"I'm sure he is." Lucy smiled faintly, then pulled her poodle forward to be introduced as well.

"Charmed, I'm sure," Brent said graciously, doffing an imaginary hat as he bent down to make Duncan's acquaintance and, in spite of herself, Lucy giggled.

Then the instructor was stepping to the middle of the room, clapping her hands loudly several times to call the class to order, and their conversation was brought to a close.

"Wait for me afterward?" Brent asked as they each began to move away toward their assigned places in the size-graduated line. Looking back at him, Lucy nodded slowly, then turned away once more, sandwiching herself between a collie and a Labrador and devoting her attention to the trainer.

Later, as she prepared for bed, Lucy looked back over the evening with satisfaction. At the session's end, she and Brent had met and gone out for coffee, spending a delightful hour discovering an easy camaraderie, which extended beyond their mutual interest in dogs. When, at the end, he had asked if she would like to accompany him to a dog show the following weekend, Lucy had agreed readily.

At last, she thought, snuggling in beneath the warmth of her down comforter, I'm finally on the right track. With Brent, she would find the relationship she had always dreamed of, and at the same time, be able to put Simon Farlow out of her mind once and for all. What could possibly be better?

Sunday was a bright, clear day, and unseasonably warm for mid-November, a fact Lucy took as a harbinger of good things to come. Brent arrived to pick her up promptly at ten, once again impeccably dressed as he had been on the night they met. Today he was wearing a burgundy cashmere sweater, pleated gray flannel slacks and a pair of tassel loafers. Seeing him, Lucy could only hope that her own outfit was up to his standard. Appearances were quite important to him, she'd gathered the other night, realizing from the comments he'd made about some of the other handlers in their class that he was not the type to appreciate a woman who looked less than her best. No sweatsuits or sneakers for this man! Lucy had thought, making a mental note, and today she had chosen her clothes with care: a pair of camel corduroy pants and a creamy, cowl-necked sweater, topped by a brown tweed hacking jacket. When she greeted him at the door, Brent's smile was warm and approving, and Lucy relaxed, prepared to enjoy their day together to the fullest.

Over the course of the next eight hours, she learned

more about dogs than she would ever have dreamed possible. In fact, she decided wryly, she learned even more than she had ever wanted to know.

Since it was almost winter, the show was being held indoors at a nearby armory. Over a thousand dogs, representing dozens of different breeds, were present, and if Lucy had thought the training class was chaos, it was nothing compared to what she saw now. Brent, however, was unperturbed. At the gate, he stopped and bought her a catalogue, then set about introducing her to the world of the dog show. With utmost patience, he explained the ins and outs of the intricate judging system and the standards of perfection against which the various breeds were judged; by the end of the day, she felt fairly well versed, if not thoroughly knowledgeable, in the art of showing dogs.

It had been fun, she reflected in the car on the way home, a nice, if not exactly stimulating, day in many ways. Brent had made a very pleasant companion. He was kind, patient and very solicitous—a man with whom she could be content, who accepted what she chose to give without always demanding more.

Pricked by a small, niggling feeling of doubt, Lucy quashed her reaction irritably. So what if no sparks seemed to fly between them? Her short-lived relationship with Simon had been very explosive, and look where that had gotten her! No, she decided, this was how truly meaningful relationships were meant to be—quiet and fulfilling, a steady flame that would last for a lifetime and not burn out overnight in one single burst of spontaneous combustion.

It was already late afternoon by the time Brent's black Trans Am pulled into her driveway. Letting the car glide to a halt, he took it out of gear and flipped off the ignition, then turned in his seat to face her. Sliding one arm along the top of the backrest behind them, Brent reached up with the other to stroke the side of her face gently from brow to jaw with the tip of his finger.

"You are a very beautiful woman, Lucy," he said huskily, "and I am a man who appreciates rare beauty."

As if mesmerized, Lucy watched his lips descend toward hers. Her eyelids fluttered shut in anticipation of his touch, but it never came, for at that moment, a loud knock sounded on the glass window just behind her head, startling them both. Immediately Brent jerked away, and Lucy turned around to see what was the matter, then stiffened.

"Good evening," Simon said cheerfully, stepping back to pull open her door then help her out of the car, without once stopping to consider whether she wanted to get out or not. "I just happened to be jogging by when I saw the car pull up, and I knew you'd never forgive me if I didn't stop in and say hello!"

The grin he gave her was ingenuously sincere, but Lucy wasn't fooled for a moment. Just jogging by, my foot! she thought angrily. The road she lived on was a dead end. How was he going to explain away that one? But before she had a chance to ask, Simon had walked right on past her, his brown eyes twinkling merrily as he extended his hand to Brent, who had hopped out as well and was now coming around the front of the car.

"Simon Farlow," he announced, "and you must be . . ."

"Brent Connors," the other man supplied readily, his manners every bit as impeccable as his clothes, although it was obvious he was somewhat confused. "Are you and Lucy neighbors?"

"Just about," Simon replied smoothly, his vague wave in the direction of Weed Street blithely dismissing the two-mile distance between the two houses. "I live over there."

Try as she might, Lucy could not ignore the way her

heart had suddenly begun to flutter almost painfully in her breast. God, he was gorgeous! Even dressed in a slouchy gray sweatsuit and a pair of well-scuffed running shoes, he was maddeningly sexy. The last rays of the setting sun brought out the golden highlights in his dark blond hair and softly outlined the contours of his very powerful, very masculine body, and Lucy could not take her eyes off him.

Turning, Simon observed her scrutiny and treated her to a dazzling smile that immediately destroyed all her defenses, yet perversely, made her all the angrier. Thoughts like these would get her nowhere!

"Well, *neighbor*, Brent and I were just about to go inside," she said sweetly, but her tone was edged in steel. "Isn't it about time you were jogging along?"

"Oh, I'm in no hurry," Simon replied easily. "Actually I seem to have developed a bit of a cramp in my leg, and I was hoping you might be able to give me a lift home." Without waiting for an invitation, he preceded them to the front step, and Lucy viewed his slight limp with a decidedly cynical eye. "But I don't mind waiting," he added, in the tone of one who is doing his utmost to make himself agreeable.

"Of course, you don't want to tax yourself if your muscles are already cramping up," Brent agreed somberly, and Lucy could cheerfully have kicked him *and* his good manners. "Why don't you come in and join us for a cup of coffee?"

"Thanks, I'd love to." Simon grinned as Lucy fumbled nervously with the key. "But if you've never had Lucy's coffee before, I think it's only fair to warn you, you're taking your life in your hands."

"Oh?" Brent said with a faint frown.

Finally the latch gave, and the door swung open.

"Nonsense," Lucy assured him airily. She reached out to link her arm through her date's and led him into the

163

living room. "I've never killed anyone yet. Now if you two would like to make yourselves comfortable, I'll get the coffee started and be right back."

In the kitchen, Lucy worked with the speed of one possessed. She didn't dare leave them alone in there together for very long. Who knew what Simon might get up to next? She didn't trust that man any farther than she could throw him!

When she returned to the living room only moments later, it was to find Simon sprawled out comfortably on the couch, his every action indicating that he had a right to make himself at home. Brent was leaning down to peer closely at the collection of family photographs on her shelf. Abruptly Lucy gulped. Some of those pictures were years old. In fact, none were very recent, and in every single one she resembled nothing so much as a beached whale!

It didn't take more than one guess to figure out who had put Brent up to such a close inspection! Lucy thought. Angrily she turned on Simon, glaring at him in stony silence, but he simply looked up at her and shrugged, his tawny brown eyes round with innocence.

Unexpectedly Brent chuckled, and Lucy moved closer to see what had caught his eye. "God!" he yelped, pointing to one of the shots. "Who's this load of blubber?"

The burst of relief Lucy felt upon realizing that he hadn't recognized her was short-lived. She wasn't out of the woods yet, not by a long shot!

"She's er . . ." she stammered, thinking fast, "er . . . she's an old friend." Pointedly she glared at Simon, daring him to contradict her.

Smoothly he rose to his feet and joined them by the shelf. "A very *good* friend, wouldn't you say?" he asked, eyes glinting wickedly.

Brent looked up at the two of them in surprise. "So

you knew her as well? I didn't realize that you and Lucy had known each other for that long."

"Oh yes, we've known each other for quite some time," Simon lied blatantly as he moved in closer to stand beside her. "We're very close, Lucy and I, aren't we, darling?"

Darling? she fumed, feeling as though she was about to explode. Darling! In all the time she'd known him, he'd never once before called her that, and she was damned if he'd start now!

Fluidly she eluded his grasp, taking several steps back and away. "Actually," she said, her voice saccharine sweet, "Simon and I are more like family—"

"Kissing cousins?" he interrupted her softly, so softly that Brent, who stood behind him, couldn't possibly have heard.

"Brother and sister," Lucy declared, loudly and firmly.

"I see," Brent said slowly, although it was obvious from the puzzled expression on his face that he didn't see at all.

"Good." Lucy smiled, then nodded toward the couch. "If you'd like to have a seat, I'm sure the coffee must be ready by now."

During the next half hour, Lucy had to call on every bit of self-control she possessed just to keep from leaping up off her chair and screaming at the top of her lungs like a madwoman. These two men were driving her crazy! Oh, on the surface everything seemed normal enough. She poured their coffee, and they drank it, conversing with each other readily. But after the first several minutes, they seemed to have forgotten all about her, excluding her from the conversation shamelessly as they discussed their jobs, their hobbies, even their cars, in a subtle game of one-upmanship, which left her growing angrier by the moment. They were like two male dogs, she decided crossly, sniffing around and challenging each other's supremacy as they sought to establish territorial rights. Well, she wasn't having any of it!

As soon as the coffee was finished, she cleared the cups away, then remained standing in what she hoped was a pointed invitation to leave. As usual, Brent's good manners rose to the occasion and he stood up as well, leaving only Simon still seated and looking as though he hadn't any intention of going anywhere.

"I believe you said you needed a ride, Farlow?" Brent reminded him pointedly. "There's no use in Lucy going out again when I can run you home myself."

"Thank you, Brent, that's very sweet of you," Lucy purred, though she shuddered inwardly at the thought of what mischief Simon might work on the ride home when she wasn't around to keep an eye on him. "Ask him to tell you about Tess," she prompted, hoping for the best. "His golden retriever has a litter of puppies due soon."

"Is that so?" Brent said politely, his tone indicating his lack of interest.

Lucy turned her attention back to Simon, who continued to lounge on the couch. "Thank you for stopping by, Simon," she said formally. Reaching down, she took his hand, then braced herself backward to all but pull him to his feet. "It was nice seeing you again."

"My pleasure." Simon grinned. He followed them out to the door, then leaned against the doorjamb insolently, watching as they said good-bye.

"I'll call you," Brent promised, bending down self-consciously to brush a quick kiss across her lips.

"Please do," Lucy murmured invitingly. Over Brent's shoulder, she caught sight of the angry gleam in Simon's eyes and knew with certainty that she had just succeeded in squeezing the tiger's tail.

Brent called again early in the week, and they chatted together amicably for several moments before making a dinner date for the following Saturday night. No sooner had she hung up the phone in her office than it rang again. This time it was Simon.

"Hello," she said coolly, sitting back in her chair and propping her feet up on the desk in a most unladylike way.

"You don't sound too pleased to hear from me," Simon growled, and Lucy wondered how he managed to convey so much injured pride through a telephone line.

"Why should I be? The last time I saw you, you embarrassed me horribly."

"Come, come now, that wasn't all my fault," Simon said soothingly. "After all, I could hardly have known that you would go so far as to disown yourself."

"So you did put him up to looking at those pictures!" Lucy cried, her suspicions confirmed.

What might have been a chuckle was quickly stifled as Simon said cheerfully, "Let's just say I pointed him in the right direction."

He sounded smug, Lucy realized suddenly, and all at once she found herself wondering what other tricks he might have been up to. "Did you and Brent have a nice ride home?"

"Very." Simon's reply gave nothing away.

"What did you two find to talk about?" she asked, her voice bland, nonchalant.

"Nothing much," Simon said, carefully matching her tone. "This and that."

"Simon . . . !"

"Actually, I told Connors that he should let you cook him dinner sometime—that it would be a real learning experience."

I should have known as much, thought Lucy, sighing with resignation. "And what did he say to that?"

For a moment, there was no answer on the line at all.

"Well?" she prompted.

"To that," Simon bit out, "he said that some women were so lovely that asking for anything else from them would be like gilding the lily."

"How nice of him to say so." Lucy smiled into the phone.

"Nice!" Simon exploded. "If he'd shoveled it on any thicker, roses would have sprouted!"

Still smiling, Lucy pretended to pout. "Are you saying you don't find me attractive, Simon?"

"Of course not!"

"Then what exactly are you trying to say?" she inquired mildly.

"That I want to see you this weekend," Simon growled, his patience obviously wearing thin.

"Sorry," Lucy said blithely, "but I already have a date."

"For the whole weekend?" His tone conveyed his outrage, and she couldn't resist baiting him just a little.

"Maybe."

Vehemently, Simon swore under his breath. When he spoke again, his voice was clipped, devoid of emotion. "All right, if that's the way you want to play it. I'll say one thing for you, Slim, you're a fast learner."

Abruptly, before there was time to reply, the line clicked dead in her ear. He'd hung up on her, Lucy realized, and the moment her outrage subsided, she decided it was probably just as well. For once in her life, words had deserted her. She had absolutely nothing to say.

She placed the receiver in its cradle, frowning as her eyes shimmered unexpectedly with unshed tears, and Lucy knew that it was his casual use of the endearment that had caused her undoing.

"Who cares what he thinks anyway?" She sniffed and squared her shoulders. Things were better this way, she knew they were. She had Brent, the man of her dreams, and Simon had his cast of thousands, so what did they need each other for anyway?

But as she leaned back into her chair, one tear overflowed and rolled slowly down her cheek, and Lucy couldn't help but wonder if refusing to see Simon was the right thing to do, why did she suddenly feel so miserable?

The restaurant where Brent took her was one she hadn't been to before, styled like a grand Mediterranean villa, with a dimly lit interior, plush booths and plenty of sparkling crystal. Lucy winced, however, when she saw the prices on the tasseled menu. He couldn't possibly be planning to spend that kind of money on her, could he? she mused, briefly entertaining the notion of trying to somehow offer to go dutch. Tact had never been her strong point, but still . . . Then, frowning, she pushed the thought aside. No, from what she knew of Brent, the very idea would offend him to the core. If he had brought her here trying to make a good impression, then the best thing she could do was sit back and pretend to be wildly impressed.

As the evening wore on, however, it became more and more difficult. Although the maitre d' and the sommelier were suitably aloof as befit their stations, and the waiter obsequious almost to the point of fawning, the food, when it arrived, was a terrible disappointment.

Too bad they hadn't taken some of the money spent on personnel and decor and put it into the kitchen where it belonged, thought Lucy, fighting to suppress a smile. If Simon were here, he and I would probably be having a good laugh over that thought right now. . . .

Abruptly, Lucy's amusement vanished. It was disconcerting the way thoughts of Simon popped into her mind at odd moments—disconcerting and *irritating*, and it had to stop!

Deliberately turning all her attention on Brent, Lucy favored him with a dazzling smile. Their conversation picked up once more, and she forced herself to match his gay, lighthearted mood. A cheerful feeling of compatibility carried them through the rest of the meal, and then they were driving home to his apartment for a nightcap.

He lived on the second floor of a red-brick, Colonial-style apartment complex, Lucy discovered, taking in every aspect of her surroundings with interest. Just what she would have expected from a man of his conservative tastes. However, when Brent opened the door to his apartment and then led her inside, she found a surprise within that she had not counted on at all. He lived in a studio! The room was large to be sure, with several big windows, and the kitchen, which ran along one wall, was hidden behind a beautiful Oriental screen. Nevertheless, it was still only one room, and Lucy could not ignore the fact that by stepping into his living room, she had entered his bedroom as well; a fact that was underscored by the commanding presence of a king-sized water bed, which she supposed was meant to double as a couch, for it provided the only seating arrangement in the room.

"You know Brutus, of course," said Brent, reaching down to pat the Great Dane who had ambled over to meet them at the door.

"Of course," Lucy echoed faintly as Brent helped her off with her coat, then hung it in the closet.

"Have a seat," he invited, waving grandly toward the bed. "I'll fix us a drink. Is brandy all right?"

"Fine." Lucy smiled wanly as she walked across the room.

Standing beside the water bed, she stared down at it dubiously. She'd heard of them, of course, even seen them, but she'd never been on one before. Somehow, this did not seem like the ideal time for her first experience! Still, there were no chairs in the room, and she couldn't very well sit on the floor. Nothing ventured, nothing gained, Lucy decided with a shrug, as she lowered herself downward gingerly, trying to balance most of her weight on the narrow wooden frame rather than the water-filled mattress itself. The attempt wasn't entirely successful, however, and she soon found herself sliding backward as the bed dipped and rocked beneath her in a way she didn't find the slightest bit endearing.

To make matters worse, Brutus chose this time to get friendly, settling down on the floor beside her, the bulk of his two-hundred-pound body resting on top of her legs and feet. Lucy shifted beneath him uncomfortably, trying to rescue her trapped limbs, but all to no avail. Finally, in desperation, she braced both hands against the dog's shoulder and gave a mighty shove. The push might have toppled a lesser dog, but not Brutus, whose only response was to turn his head and peer at her reproachfully, then reach out and lick her arm from wrist to elbow with his great slobbering tongue.

"Good, I see you two have made friends already." Brent chuckled, sounding enormously pleased, as he ducked back out around the screen carrying two snifters full of amber liquid. "I hoped you would. Brutus doesn't take to all the . . . er, friends I bring home. But I knew right away that you were something special."

"Go on, boy," he instructed the dog, and Brutus heaved himself up and shambled away reluctantly.

Lucy's feeling of relief was short-lived, however, for no sooner had Brutus vacated the spot than Brent took his place, sitting down so close beside her that the entire length of their bodies from shoulder to thigh touched in a way that could hardly have been accidental.

"What a nice apartment," she said politely, trying unobtrusively to shift her weight away as the water bed rolled and gurgled beneath them once more. Taking the glass Brent held out to her, she raised it to her lips for a hasty sip, and felt somewhat reassured by the liquid warmth flowing suddenly through her veins.

"What do you think?" Brent asked, patting the huge bed enthusiastically. "Isn't this great?"

Lucy smiled faintly. "Actually," she admitted, "I've never been on a water bed before." The sip she took this time was closer to a gulp.

"Take my word for it," Brent said, beaming, "you're going to love it!"

At that thought, Lucy tipped back her glass and polished off the rest of her brandy. There was no time to indulge her growing doubts, however, for at that moment, Brent set his drink down on the floor and reached over to gather her into his arms. Giving herself up to the embrace, Lucy closed her eyes and surrendered, prepared to experience once again the rapture she had felt in Simon's arms.

But to her dismay, this time around nothing seemed right. Brent's mouth felt hot and wet and heavy upon her own, his touch rough and demanding, invading rather than inviting. She parted her lips, and his tongue slipped inside, but the sensation was not erotic, merely intrusive. Bewildered, Lucy pulled her head back and away, exposing the smooth line of her throat, which Brent dipped down to nuzzle happily, oblivious to her lack of response.

Head tilted back as she took several deep, calming breaths, Lucy's eyelids opened and she found herself staring up at the ceiling, its blank, white expanse not at all conducive to the surging, pounding emotions she wanted to be feeling. Deliberately she snapped her eyes shut, trying hard to concentrate as Brent's hand began to roam slowly over her body. Maybe the problem was that his technique was somewhat different than Simon's, she told herself firmly. Maybe all she needed was some time to switch gears and get used to the difference.

"Mmm," she murmured, trying valiantly to work up some passion or even some enthusiasm. "This is nice." Nice? her mind screamed back at her in denial. Listen to yourself! You sound like a woman examining products at a Tupperware party!

"Yes, it is," Brent agreed softly. Bracing his hands against her shoulders, he pushed her gently backward, and Lucy immediately discovered that the soft, rolling mattress provided no support for resistance. Before she knew it, she was lying down, her feet having somehow left the floor as the water bed rocked beneath her. To her amazement, she found herself rolling toward the center of the mattress, her dress hiking itself up alarmingly about her thighs with each revolution.

"Brent, wait, I . . ." Where had he gotten so many hands from all of a sudden? Lucy wondered dimly, trying in vain to capture and contain the fingers now roaming over her body in bold conquest.

"Not now, baby," Brent growled as his hands moved around to the zipper on the back of her dress. "We'll talk later."

Arching beneath him, Lucy twisted away, wondering as she did so whether or not it was possible to become seasick on dry land. Too late she realized that the move, while denying him access to her zipper, had the unwelcome effect of thrusting her breasts upward right underneath Brent's nose. Gazing down at her, his eyes smoldering with desire, he muttered thickly, "Sure, babe, if that's what you want, I'll—"

Whatever it was he had in mind, Lucy never found out, for at that moment, she heard a low growl followed by a jealous whine as Brutus, who obviously didn't like being ignored, galloped across the room and leaped up to join them on the bed. One moment she had been lying firmly entwined in Brent's embrace, and the next she found herself flying rather inelegantly through the air as the backlash created by the massive dog's sudden pounce on the mattress catapulted her up and off the bed. Landing half on the frame and half on the floor, Lucy scrambled quickly to her feet.

"Brutus, damn it! Get off the bed!" Brent roared, and Lucy knew that if the whole situation hadn't been so awful, she could have found it quite hilariously funny.

"Don't move him on my account," she announced, stooping down and picking up her shoes, then slipping them on.

"What do you mean?" Brent cried. Then realization dawned, and his voice grew angry. "Hey, where are you going? You can't leave now!"

Unaccountably, it was Simon's voice Lucy heard, and her features softened as she remembered his gentle words: "Don't you know that the only person you ever have to please is yourself?"

"I can, and I am," she said coolly, retrieving her coat from the closet. Glancing back she saw that Brent was still lying prone on the bed, his face wearing an expression of petulant disbelief like a child who'd just found out he was going to be denied his favorite toy.

Good God! thought Lucy, blessing the Great Dane's timing. What am I doing here? I must have been out of my mind!

With that thought, she turned her back on the man of her dreams and walked out the door.

10

It was a marvelous exit, thought Lucy. It had dignity and great style. But in the way of most grand gestures, it wasn't perfect.

By the time she reached the street below, Lucy was well aware of its major flaw—she had no means of transportation and, as it was after midnight and she was in the middle of New Canaan's quiet residential section, no means of calling for any either. The mile-and-a-half walk to the railroad station left her cold and tired, her ankles aching from the abuse dished out by her flimsy, spike-heeled sandals. One lone cabbie was in attendance, and she climbed into the car gratefully, only too pleased to pay an exorbitant sum to be carried the remaining two miles home.

The following week was blessedly hectic. Between her work, the ongoing training classes for Duncan, and then another session with Sally Bonnel, Lucy had plenty to keep her busy. All that, however, was not enough to hold her thoughts at bay, and she found herself spending a great deal of time trying to figure out how it was possible that her life, which had always been so sane and simple and secure, could have become so complicated, so quickly. And when in the end, she finally figured out what was wrong, it happened quite by accident. Thursday night, she arrived home from work late. What was supposed to have been a quick stop at the supermarket to pick up some yogurt had somehow turned into a half-hour shopping spree. Dumping the two full brown paper bags down on the counter, she took off her coat and tossed it over a chair, then turned back to unpack the groceries.

I could feed an army with this, Lucy mused, frowning in dismay as she restocked the refrigerator. And this was the third time she'd stopped for food this week!

"I've been watching what I eat all right," she muttered to herself disgustedly, "watching everything in sight disappear straight into my mouth!"

The groceries put away, Lucy mixed up a bowl of food for Duncan and set it down on the floor, then picked up a package of Twinkies and wandered into the living room. It just isn't fair, she decided crossly, as she unwrapped the cakes. Why was it that the heroines in all the novels she'd ever read always *lost* their appetites when they were thwarted in love? They wasted away to nothing, while she . . .

Abruptly, Lucy brought herself up short. Love? she thought incredulously. Was that what this was all about?

With a small moan, she sank down onto the couch, drawing her knees up under her chin and wrapping her arms securely about her legs. What a fool she had been not to realize what was happening! All the while she'd spent searching for true love and the man of her dreams, both had been right within her grasp, but she'd been too blind to see it! If only she hadn't been so busy trying to rationalize everything—so determined to think with her head that she had refused to listen to her heart.

She'd never meant to fall in love with Simon, certainly never expected it to happen, and in the end, she hadn't even recognized the emotion. What a laugh! thought Lucy, but her lips drew downward in a frown. The irony of the situation was that the joke was on her. She'd been so sure all along that the man she'd fall in love with would be perfect, or nearly so. And Simon wasn't even close! He made fun of her cooking and her clothes, couldn't teach tennis worth a damn and he had a little black book that had to belong in the Guinness book of records. She'd been expecting her knight to wear shining armor, not a sweatsuit and an old pair of running shoes. No wonder she'd been confused!

Closing her eyes, Lucy leaned back wearily against the plump cushions as Duncan climbed up onto the couch beside her. The telltale sound of crackling paper alerted her to the fact that he was investigating her discarded Twinkies, but suddenly she didn't have the energy to care.

So she was in love with Simon Farlow, was she? Well, that was just grand! Especially that she should discover it now of all times, after she had finally succeeding in slamming the door in his face one time too many. He had tried to make up with her, tried to get her to give their relationship another chance, and she had pushed him away, telling herself that she knew what was best. Hah! Lucy thought disgustedly. The only thing that was clear was that she didn't know very much of anything! Whatever chance she might have had with Simon was gone now.

It was one thing to tell yourself that life goes on, Lucy discovered over the next few days, quite another to make it happen. On Saturday night, when the first real blizzard of the season blew in full force, she welcomed the diversion. She'd make something really terrific for dinner, she decided, wandering out to the kitchen. Then, after she'd eaten, she would turn off all the lights indoors and sit down to watch and enjoy the quiet, majestic beauty of the winter storm.

Opening the refrigerator door, she pulled a breadstick off the top shelf and popped it into her mouth as she bent down for a closer look at the possibilities. Feeling a sharp pinch, Lucy straightened abruptly, a flash of irritation creasing her brow. These jeans weren't this tight last week, were they? she wondered, frowning. Granted, designer jeans were meant to fit closely, but *this* closely? Reaching down, she slipped her fingers inside the waistband and tugged on it gently. It didn't give an inch. Great, just great, she thought. Now, on top of everything else, she was gaining weight! When was the last time she had been on a scale anyway?

Stepping back, Lucy slammed the refrigerator door, turning away empty-handed. "That's it!" she muttered aloud. "This time, that's really it. I've had it!"

Bad enough that Simon had invaded her heart and her thoughts, but now he was having an effect on her body, too. Well, that was one insult she wasn't going to take lying down!

Who was she trying to kid anyway, with all that noble talk about life going on? Lucy thought irritably. Love wasn't something one waited to get over, like a disease. She didn't want to get over Simon, damn it! She wanted to go to him, to be with him. . . .

Frowning, she thought back over the past several weeks, the images flickering quickly through her mind. She'd been wrong at almost every turn, she could see that now. Because all her talk of ideals and doing what was best had been nothing more than a sham, a coverup.

The truth of the matter was that she'd been just plain scared. Scared to compete for Simon for fear that she might not measure up. Scared, deep down inside, that she was still that same fat little kid who didn't stand a chance.

Well damn it, she was still scared! But she wasn't about to lose something as important as this because of it!

No, thought Lucy with a sudden burst of self-confidence, she hadn't taken control of her life successfully once, only to relinquish it the first time things got tough. She'd learned to have enough respect for her body not to abuse it by overeating, and now she was finally learning that she had enough respect for herself not to let Simon go, not at least without putting up one hell of a fight!

He might very well reject her love, and it might even be exactly what she deserved. But at least she was going to give herself that chance. She was going to stand up for herself and lay her feelings right on the line, and if after that, Simon still turned her away, then she'd—then she'd just have to come up with a way to change his mind!

Quickly, before she had a chance to lose her nerve, Lucy picked up the phone on the wall and dialed Simon's number. Please God, she prayed, not the answering machine, not now, not tonight! She drew in her breath, then held it as the phone rang three, then four times. Finally, at the fifth ring, when she was just about to give up, the receiver was snatched up on the other end.

"Hello!" Simon snapped, sounding harried and quite breathless, and immediately Lucy was sure she'd picked a terrible time to call.

"Simon?" she said, her voice tentative. "It's Lucy."

"Slim, thank God!" Simon breathed. "I'm in terrible trouble. You've got to help me!"

"Of course," Lucy replied, her eyes opening wide in

surprise. Whatever she had expected his response to be, it certainly wasn't this! "What's the matter?"

"It's Tess, she's having her puppies. I've read all the books, I thought I was prepared, but now I'm not so sure. I'm afraid something's gone wrong. Slim, there's blood everywhere."

"I don't think that necessarily means something's wrong," Lucy said soothingly, wanting to reach out and reassure him through the wire as she tried in vain to remember any pertinent facts she might know about reproduction. "How is Tess doing? Is she nervous or upset?"

"She seems agitated. She's pacing around in the whelping box and she keeps panting."

"Have you tried calling the vet?"

"The local man isn't on call tonight. His service referred me to a twenty-four-hour clinic in Norwalk, but in this weather I'd never be able to get her there. Slim, you've got to come. I can't go through this alone!"

"Of course I'll come," Lucy agreed immediately. "I don't know how bad the roads are. It may take ten or fifteen minutes, but I shouldn't be any longer than that."

"No!" Simon snapped. "I don't want you to drive. Stay there and bundle up. I'll be right over to get you."

No amount of argument could change Simon's mind, and in the end Lucy decided it was easier to simply let him have his way. Ten minutes later when the Porsche arrived, she was waiting by the front door, swathed in layers of down; ten minutes after that, they had made it back to his house. Hurrying inside, Simon led the way up the spiral staircase to the second floor.

"Where on earth is Tess having these puppies?" Lucy asked somewhat breathlessly as she trotted along behind, her much shorter legs having a hard time keeping up with his long stride.

"In the guest bedroom," Simon said, grinning boyishly. "Considering how much I've been looking forward to their arrival, I thought it was only fitting."

Entering the brightly lit room, Lucy immediately saw the low-sided, wooden whelping box Simon had set up in the corner. There, Tess lay on her side, nursing three small golden puppies.

"Good," said Simon, peering into the box quickly, then stepping even more hastily away. "She hasn't had any more while I was gone."

"She seems to be doing all right," Lucy said uncertainly. She knelt down beside the box for a closer look. Simon had been right about one thing, there did seem to be a great deal of blood everywhere.

"Seems to be?" he cried, his agitation obvious. "What do you mean, seems to be? Don't you know?"

"Of course not." Lucy shook her head. "Why should I?"

"But I thought women knew all about these things!"

Lucy shot him a withering glance. "I suppose they might if they've had children of their own," she said drily, "but as far as having babies is concerned, I've got no more experience than you do."

"Terrific." Simon moaned.

Frowning, Lucy thought for a moment, then brightened. "But I think I might know someone who does."

Simon looked at her hopefully. "Your mother?" he guessed.

"No, not my mother," Lucy replied with a laugh. "I'm afraid puppies are a little foreign to her as well. No, Tess deserves only the best. We'll go right to the source—the woman who sold me Duncan. She's been breeding poodles forever. We've stayed in touch over the years, and I'm sure she won't mind my calling. Don't worry, I'll bet anything she'll know exactly what to do."

"This way," said Simon, leading her to the nearest phone. The call was soon accomplished, taking no more than a matter of minutes as Lucy jotted down a quick set of notes, then hurried back to join Simon and Tess in the guest room.

"Everything is fine," she assured him quickly and was pleased to see the lines of concern furrowing his brow soften and relax. "I described the situation to her, and she said Tess seems to be doing a great job. All that blood and gore is perfectly normal. We're to change the towels underneath her periodically so that the box stays clean and dry, but other than that, we're just to let her get on with it."

Throughout the night, they kept careful watch over Tess's progress, monitoring the birth of the remaining puppies. Lucy spent the night on her knees beside the box where she was in a position to reach in and lend a hand if necessary, sometimes cutting an umbilical cord or disposing of an afterbirth when Tess became harried and confused, and once, cleaning the fluid out of the nose and lungs of a puppy who wasn't breathing properly. Simon maintained a position of relative safety on the other side of the room. After several attempts at drawing him closer, Lucy finally realized that he was more than willing to help, as long as he did not have to come near enough to actually see what was going on. After that, Simon was relegated to the behind-the-scenes work—supplying stack after stack of clean towels, brewing several pots of hot tea and, when nothing else was needed, pacing back and forth across the room with the time-honored dedication of all expectant fathers.

Finally, by three o'clock in the morning, the job was done. Leaning against the side of the low, wooden box, Tess lay back in satisfied exhaustion as Lucy lined up the eight tiny, golden puppies for their first proper meal. "Come and look," she whispered, walking over and taking Simon's hand to lead him back to the corner for a glimpse of Tess's new family.

Together, they knelt down on the floor beside the box, watching the scene in silence for several moments, until Simon reached out tentatively to stroke one of the small, furry bodies. "They're beautiful," he breathed, his voice filled with awe, "truly magnificent."

Entranced by the quiet, tender beauty of the moment, Lucy only smiled. Simon rocked back on his heels, then turned to face her. "And so are you," he murmured. His hand came up and he traced the side of her face with his fingertips.

Lucy gasped softly, drawing a quick, unexpected breath at the way the simple caress seemed to set her skin on fire and fill her soul with longing. She trembled involuntarily, and a sudden light smoldered in Simon's sable brown eyes as he towered over her, his expression one of devastating awareness. All at once, the slight distance between them seemed unbearable, and when Simon moved forward to close the gap, his hands reaching out to pull her to him, Lucy melted eagerly, joyously, into the embrace.

He covered her mouth with his, the touch of his lips warm and supple, and Lucy moaned softly, opening her mouth and drawing him closer still as she welcomed his tongue with her own. Pressing her body to his, she felt the strong, pulsing tempo of his heart and knew that he was just as deeply affected by the kiss as she. He must still feel something for her, Lucy thought, warmed by the knowledge. Now if only he would give her another chance!

Drawing back, Simon cupped her head tenderly with his hands, his fingers tangling in her hair, and Lucy tilted her head back into his palms and gazed up at him warmly. Though they'd been together all evening, and the poignant beauty of the miracle they had just shared had gone a long way toward breaking down the barriers between them, she knew there was still a great deal that remained unsaid.

"We must talk," she whispered, hating to break the magical spell surrounding them but knowing that it must be done.

Simon nodded in agreement, then rose to his feet, pulling her up beside him. "She deserves a rest," he said, nodding toward Tess. "Why don't we go downstairs?"

In the living room, he left her sitting on the couch, then walked around to turn off all the lights one by one, until he finally came to the last switch on the wall and flicked on the outdoor floodlights, illuminating with stunning clarity the majestic storm that still raged outside. When he joined her on the couch, Simon reached out to pull her to him once more, but this time Lucy resisted, shaking her head slowly. She would give herself to him again, joyously and completely, but not before she had said the things that had to be said. She loved Simon with all her heart and soul, and it was important that there be no misunderstandings left between them.

"I've missed you," she murmured, not quite knowing where to begin. Tilting her head back, she gazed up at him, the love she felt shining luminously in her eyes. "I've missed you terribly, Simon, and I've been such a fool. You offered me the chance to reform you once, and if the offer's still open . . ."

Simon opened his mouth to speak, but Lucy laid her forefinger gently over his lips to silence him, knowing she needed to finish what she had to say before she lost her nerve. "I know that you don't feel the same way I do. You may not love me now, but in time—"

"I don't need any time," said Simon. He parted his lips, then used his tongue to draw her finger into his mouth and suck on it gently. "But I'm afraid that particular offer's been withdrawn—"

"Simon, no!" The small, anguished cry seemed to have been drawn from the depths of her very soul, and this time it was Simon's hand that reached up to silence and reassure her.

"As it turns out," he confessed, "I've already done the job myself. You see, once I'd met you, I just wasn't interested in anybody else."

Lucy's eyes opened in wonder as she took in what Simon had just said. "You wouldn't be handing me a line, would you?" she asked cautiously.

Simon's lips twitched briefly as though he were undecided whether to smile or frown. "Is my reputation really that bad?" he demanded.

"Worse," Lucy affirmed solemnly, but all at once she was filled with a heady, breathless feeling of elation, and she had to bite down hard on her lower lip in order to keep a straight face. "New Canaan's own Casanova, that's what you are."

Slowly Simon shook his head. "Don't tell me we've had that between us as well," he said, frowning. "Slim, don't you know that men who enter their thirties without having married are automatically labeled playboys? It comes with the territory, but that doesn't make it so."

"Oh, I don't think I'm going to mind being in love with a playboy," Lucy said teasingly. "Actually I find the prospect rather exciting."

"Exciting, is it?" Simon growled. "I'll show you excitement!" His lips swooped down to capture hers, moving over them hungrily, fervidly, in a kiss whose heated urgency left them clinging to one another breathlessly.

"There is one small thing," Lucy murmured when they had finally drawn apart.

"Yes?"

"About the blond bimbos . . . ?" Lucy's voice trailed away expressively.

Unexpectedly Simon grinned. "So they got to you, did

they? I hoped they would. I never in my whole life had less fun taking so many different ladies to so many different places, all in the hope that we'd be spotted by someone who would relay the word back to you!"

For a moment, Lucy could only glare at him in outrage, then reluctantly she grinned as well. "In that case, you have Margo to thank, because she's the one who passed along the news."

"The ex–best friend?"

Lucy waved one hand airily. "She's been reinstated."

"And were you devastated?"

"Yes and no," Lucy said slowly, considering her reply. "I was certainly unhappy, and terribly angry at you, too. But at the time I hadn't yet realized that I was in love with you. All I knew was that my whole life was in turmoil, and I couldn't figure out why."

"*Your* life was in turmoil!" Simon cried. "How do you think I felt? You were driving me crazy. Everything was just so much fun and games with you. I could never figure out where I stood. And for a man who's used to calling the shots in his relationships, that can be very hard to take!"

"You didn't seem confused," Lucy pointed out. "In fact, if anything, you were too cool, too much in control —like that night after we made love, and you very calmly got up and went home. Now that," she said slowly, "was when I was devastated."

"Oh, Slim," Simon murmured, gathering her close. "I never wanted to hurt you, but I had to leave that night, don't you see? It threw me terribly to discover that it was your first time. I was overwhelmed. I've never felt like that before. I wanted to make everything wonderful for you, to hold you in my arms and reassure you of my love. Then you as much as told me that what we had just shared meant nothing to you, and I couldn't believe it. I needed time to think. When you reached for me again, I knew I should have held you away, but I just couldn't. I was already in over my head. The truth of the matter is that if I had spent the night in that bed, slept with you nestled in my arms and awakened with you beside me in the morning, I knew that I would never be able to let you go."

"Oh, my poor Simon," Lucy whispered, nuzzling his neck with her lips, "I never meant to hurt you either. How little I understood then—about love, about myself, about anything!"

"I love you, Slim," Simon said softly, and Lucy felt the light, feathery touch of his lips brushing the top of her head with kisses.

Drawing her head back, she looked up at him from beneath her lowered lashes. "I love you, too."

"Oh, Slim." Simon groaned. A shudder rippled through his body, touching her as well. "You don't know how long I've waited to hear you say that. For a while, I almost gave up hope. You were so busy making light of everything we had. No matter what I did, you never seemed to take me seriously."

"I was afraid to," Lucy admitted quietly. "I've thought of you constantly over the past few weeks, but I was afraid to accept my feelings for what they really were."

"Well, I hope you suffered," Simon said wickedly, "because these past few weeks have been hell for me—missing you and needing you and wanting you—and knowing that you had to make the first move this time or things would never be right between us. I'd already tried every way I knew to convince you of what I felt, until finally I realized there was just no way I could make you believe in me until you had learned to believe in yourself. And you have now, haven't you?"

Looking up at him, Lucy nodded slowly, contentedly.

"So what do you think?" Simon asked, grinning down at her. "Will you be able to take living in a glass house? It means you'll have to settle down, you know—no more throwing stones, at yourself, or anybody else."

"Just when my aim was getting so good." Lucy sighed dramatically as she pretended to consider his offer.

"Then again," Simon said reasonably, "if this house doesn't meet with your approval, I'm sure we can come up with one that does. After all, you are going to be marrying an architect."

"Am I?" said Lucy, delicately arching one eyebrow upward.

"You most certainly are," Simon growled.

"Well, thank God for that." Lucy sighed, and she snuggled down into his arms knowing that she had finally found just the right place to be.

YOU'LL BE SWEPT AWAY WITH SILHOUETTE DESIRE

$1.75 each

1 ☐ James

2 ☐ Monet

3 ☐ Clay

4 ☐ Carey

5 ☐ Baker

6 ☐ Mallory

7 ☐ St. Claire

8 ☐ Dee

9 ☐ Simms

10 ☐ Smith

$1.95 each

11 ☐ James

12 ☐ Palmer

13 ☐ Wallace

14 ☐ Valley

15 ☐ Vernon

16 ☐ Major

17 ☐ Simms

18 ☐ Ross

19 ☐ James

20 ☐ Allison

21 ☐ Baker

22 ☐ Durant

23 ☐ Sunshine

24 ☐ Baxter

25 ☐ James

26 ☐ Palmer

27 ☐ Conrad

28 ☐ Lovan

29 ☐ Michelle

30 ☐ Lind

31 ☐ James

32 ☐ Clay

33 ☐ Powers

34 ☐ Milan

35 ☐ Major

36 ☐ Summers

37 ☐ James

38 ☐ Douglass

39 ☐ Monet

40 ☐ Mallory

41 ☐ St. Claire

42 ☐ Stewart

43 ☐ Simms

44 ☐ West

45 ☐ Clay

46 ☐ Chance

47 ☐ Michelle

48 ☐ Powers

49 ☐ James

50 ☐ Palmer

51 ☐ Lind

52 ☐ Morgan

53 ☐ Joyce

54 ☐ Fulford

55 ☐ James

56 ☐ Douglass

57 ☐ Michelle

58 ☐ Mallory

59 ☐ Powers

60 ☐ Dennis

61 ☐ Simms

62 ☐ Monet

63 ☐ Dee

64 ☐ Milan

65 ☐ Allison

66 ☐ Langtry

67 ☐ James

68 ☐ Browning

69 ☐ Carey

70 ☐ Victor

71 ☐ Joyce

72 ☐ Hart

73 ☐ St. Clair

74 ☐ Douglass

75 ☐ McKenna

76 ☐ Michelle

77 ☐ Lowell

78 ☐ Barber

79 ☐ Simms

80 ☐ Palmer

81 ☐ Kennedy

82 ☐ Clay

YOU'LL BE SWEPT AWAY WITH SILHOUETTE DESIRE

$1.95 each

83 ☐ Chance	90 ☐ Roszel	97 ☐ James	104 ☐ Chase
84 ☐ Powers	91 ☐ Browning	98 ☐ Joyce	105 ☐ Blair
85 ☐ James	92 ☐ Carey	99 ☐ Major	106 ☐ Michelle
86 ☐ Malek	93 ☐ Berk	100 ☐ Howard	107 ☐ Chance
87 ☐ Michelle	94 ☐ Robbins	101 ☐ Morgan	108 ☐ Gladstone
88 ☐ Trevor	95 ☐ Summers	102 ☐ Palmer	
89 ☐ Ross	96 ☐ Milan	103 ☐ James